ALONE IN MIAMI AT 3AM

A MILLIONAIRE ROMANCE

J. DOMINIQUE

Alone In Miami At 3AM

Mailing List

To stay up to date on new releases, plus get information on contests, sneak peeks, and more,

Go To The Website Below...

www.colehartsignature.com

ZURI ROSS

I felt like a fool. No, I felt like a *damn* fool because there was no way I'd gone against everything I knew and done the unthinkable, only for my husband to be playing in my face. My nose turned up, looking at him sleeping peacefully as our third, Erica, laid on his chest snoring and drooling. The way his arm was wrapped around her you would've thought they were the married couple and I was the one they'd invited into their bed, but that wasn't the part that had me questioning shit, even though it was playing a huge role. What was bothering me, even hours after we'd finished, was the way they were acting during the threesome. The things they were saying and the way they interacted seemed way too comfortable for two people that had just met that week.

I wanted to believe it was only my insecurities resurfacing after the past year of turmoil Deshawn and I had gone through. Between two miscarriages, my depression, and Deshawn pulling away, I honestly thought we wouldn't be able to come out of the rut we'd found ourselves in. It was like we were moving around each other and just existing in our marriage, especially once his business started picking up. I already felt like a failure being unable to carry a baby for him, but the way he shunned me only made the situation worse. When I'd bring up the distance between us, he would assure me that it wasn't intentional and that he was only trying to focus on building up his detailing business. Considering that the first few years of our marriage were spent with me paying down his debt so he could secure a business loan, I couldn't pretend like I wasn't happy that he was finally turning a real profit. He'd gone from working out of our garage to getting an actual shop and hiring a few employees. I was definitely proud of him and was thirsty to share his success with my mama and best friend Sevyn since neither approved of me paying his bills in the first place. What he was able to accomplish in the last year and us being able to go on the cruise we were currently on, made it feel like it was all worth it. When he'd surprised me with the tickets, I immediately felt like it was an opportunity for us to get back on the same page and I was willing to do anything to make things better. That was why, despite my reservations, I'd agreed to a threesome with a woman of his choosing. It was every man's fantasy and as much as I wanted him to only want me, I wasn't foolish enough to believe he was any different from any other man. Besides, if that small thing was all it would take to save our marriage, then I was willing to try.

That's how I'd gone into things feeling, and Deshawn did his best to involve me in each step, from being there to give my opinion of the woman he selected and setting rules and boundaries for during and after. Erica hadn't been my first choice though. Not only because she was at least five years younger than us, but she seemed wild and unpredictable. As beautiful as I knew I was, I also couldn't help but feel insecure around her. She was gorgeous, with flawless honey-colored skin, huge hazel eyes, a cute little button nose, and full lips that she kept glossy. The blonde lace front she wore complemented her very well and if I didn't know my lace because of Sevyn, I wouldn't have even been able to tell it hadn't grown from her scalp. The girl could've been a model if I was being honest, and while she probably could've gotten any man on this cruise she wanted, it was my husband whose attention she caught. Even though I had reservations, Deshawn was

too excited for me to back out, and now I was completely regretting it. I considered calling up Sevyn to see if maybe I was overre-
acting, but I already knew she'd curse me the fuck out for even
agreeing to this shit. As bad as I needed the advice, I was never
going to tell her ass about it. I'd just have to work this shit out on
my own. Besides, we'd be docking in Miami soon and I wouldn't
have to worry about seeing Erica again or even thinking about this
shit.

I sat at a table alone while all the other guests danced around me
having fun as they celebrated a successful trip. In less than twenty-
four hours we'd be returning to Miami and going back to our
regularly scheduled lives and I couldn't help feeling relieved. Ever
since the threesome things had been strange to say the least. I was
noticing more and more some of the funny shit I'd been ignoring
before. The entire time we'd been on the cruise, Deshawn had
pulled random disappearing acts and although I thought it was
strange, I never acknowledged them because of how few and far
between they were. Now that shit was seeming even more sketchy
and I couldn't even blame it on my own insecurities. Not only
that, but his phone was going off constantly and he'd either try to
answer it elsewhere or not at all. His excuse was always that he still
had a business to run, but I knew that was bullshit. He was being
sneaky and the only person he could have been fucking off with
was the one I'd allowed in our bed.

   As if on cue, Erica came strutting into the dining hall and a
few moments later, my husband was trailing in behind her trying
to adjust his clothes. I shook my head and scoffed, waiting to see if
he even attempted to look for me, but his attention was directed
to where Erica had gone. When he did spot her over in the corner
laughing with some tall, lanky nigga and another group of
women, his nostrils flared and he stormed in her direction. I
couldn't help thinking that in our whole seven years of being

together, he'd *never* looked so jealous. Disgusted, I finally stood while he pulled her away from the group roughly. He was so focused on her that he didn't even notice me walking up to them until it was too late.

"Why you in that nigga face laughing and shit with my dick on your breath!" he yelled right as the music paused. My heart instantly constricted in my chest and my steps faltered. Assuming was one thing, but to hear him say he was messing with this woman out loud was a slap in the face that had me ready to tear some shit up.

Since his back was to me, she saw me first, and instead of looking alarmed or even afraid like she should've, the bitch had the nerve to smirk. Deshawn quickly realized that she was focused on something over his shoulder, and he whipped around angrily until his eyes landed on me.

"So you are fuckin' her?" It was more of an acknowledgment than a question because the stupid ass look on his face told me everything I needed to know. He scratched the back of his neck uncomfortably and took a step in my direction.

"Babe, I—"

"Girl, we *been* fuckin'! You late as hell!" Erica shouted around him smugly. "You gotta be the dumbest bitch ever! Do I look like the type to randomly engage in a fuckin' threesome with some people I don't know? Think about it!"

"Aye, Erica chill," Deshawn tossed out over his shoulder, knowing better than to turn his back to me.

"No! You're over here in my face 'cause I was laughing with a nigga and your wife don't even know that you *paid* for this trip for me and my girls!" she continued ranting and spilling more tea that had me boiling on the inside. By now Deshawn was damn near wrestling with her to try and cover her mouth, but she was easily able to wiggle out of his grasp. Now common sense should've told me to remove myself from the ghetto ass scene they were making, but my feet refused to move. I was completely stunned, because while I was thinking their shit had started on this ship, she was letting me know just how wrong I was. She was still talking and giving me details I hadn't asked for as Deshawn desperately tried to get a handle on her.

"You should be trying to figure out why yo' old fat ass can't carry a baby for him instead of worrying about what the fuck we got going on!"

It seemed like everything around me stopped and my heart pounded loudly in my ears. My eyes shot to Deshawn in disbelief, and he finally stopped fighting with Erica long enough to try and reach for me. Before he could even get the words out, I slapped the shit out of him. I knew it hurt too because my hand was stinging, but that didn't stop me from doing it again and again.

"Keep yo' hands off him!"

My attention had been stuck on Deshawn's trifling ass despite the harsh words that Erica had been spewing. I wasn't even going to address her because *he* was the one that had invited her into our lives and *my* business, but she stepped in between us and tried to push me away. My height and thick frame stopped me from falling. I barely stumbled and quickly came back with an uppercut that knocked her into Deshawn. They went crashing into a table and I wasted no time walking over so I could beat their asses some more, but I was quickly hit from behind. Regaining my composure, I swung blindly instantly making contact with whoever had hit me and the fight was on. More than two bitches were trying to throw hands, but I was giving them all the business as chaos erupted around us. I didn't know who these people were, but it seemed like the whole boat was throwing punches and by the time security was able to break it up, I was sitting in cuffs along with Deshawn, Erica, and a whole bunch of others. *Fuck.*

ZURI ROSS

I magine getting kicked off a cruise for starting a brawl with a bitch you had a threesome with and your no-good ass husband. I'd spent the night locked in our cabin with security guarding the door like I was one of the poor people on the Titanic. Thankfully, they'd separated me from Deshawn because I would've been trying to fuck him up in that little ass space had they not. On the flip side, I couldn't help wondering if they had him locked up with his little hoe and unfortunately, that thought bothered me more than I cared to admit. Erica had told me a mouthful, but I still wanted to know how long they'd been messing around. Where had they even met? Had he been planning on leaving me for her?

My stomach knotted up every time that question crossed my mind and it had me ready to throw the fuck up. I'd worked my ass off to pay his debt, I'd dealt with the cold shoulder he'd given me when I was at my lowest and still found the strength to support him, and worst of all, I shared our bed with a bitch I didn't even know to satisfy him and that still wasn't enough for him. I was already humiliated enough, but then the nigga had the nerve to call out to me as I was being escorted off the ship like I was supposed to ride home with him. I pretended like I didn't even know his crazy ass, even though half the guests had witnessed our bullshit the night before, and promptly asked the men walking alongside me to keep him away. Their interference allowed me to get into a cab and I made sure to tell the Middle Eastern driver to step on it.

Now it was hours later and I was sitting in a hotel room because I refused to ride home on the same plane as Deshawn's stupid ass. I didn't even want to go home at all, but I knew I wasn't going to be able to afford the suite I was in for more than a couple days.

Groaning, I turned over and my eyes landed right on the digital clock on the nightstand. The bold, red letters let me know it was just after two in the morning, and I decided that a drink was what I needed to help me sleep since my mind wouldn't stop racing. Since I'd taken a shower before bed, I went ahead and slipped on a nude, thin-strapped one piece and a satin, floral-print kimono. Taking off my bonnet, I fluffed out my hair and fixed my bang so it covered the growing bruise that was evidence of the fight. Somehow, I had managed to walk away with just that and maybe a lump or two on my head, which was why I'd taken down my vacation braids and was rocking my natural thick coils.

As I left my suite, I ignored another call from Deshawn and immediately blocked him, but I barely made it to the elevator before my bestie Sevyn's number flashed across my screen. Sighing, I contemplated whether or not to answer. I was sure my soon-to-be ex-husband was the reason behind her calling me out of the blue, and while I normally would've wanted to talk, I was still too embarrassed. Without a doubt, Deshawn hadn't given her full details because she would've been blowing me up from behind bars for doing something crazy and not from her cell phone.

Even after going to the voicemail twice, this crazy ass girl sent a text before calling right back. It was obvious she wasn't going to give up and regardless of me not wanting to hear her mouth, I answered.

"He—"

"Oh, you better had answered or I was gone be catching the next flight then an Uber to..." she paused briefly before spouting off the hotel's address. Rolling my eyes, I climbed onto the first elevator that wasn't full of drunk clubgoers.

"I really hate I shared my location with yo' ass," I grumbled, making her cackle wryly.

"That's what besties do, hoe! Now why is yo' child calling *me* of all people trying to find out where you are? I thought y'all were supposed to be coming back today? What his goofy ass do now?" she shot off question after question, and I sighed. The insult toward Deshawn didn't go unnoticed. Normally, I would've defended him, but I didn't have it in me to go up for him at the moment. Sevyn hated his guts and she never missed an opportunity to let me know it, along with my mama. My father, on the other hand, was the only one who actually acted as if he liked Deshawn, but he was so hung up on the illustrious idea of black love that he didn't care what a nigga did as long as he was a "good black man." Clearly, that wasn't my husband though, because a good man wouldn't do half the shit Deshawn had.

"Friend I—" My voice cracked as hurt overshadowed the anger I'd just been feeling a second before.

"Oh hell naw! It's that bad?" she gasped.

"Worse," I managed to get out, dropping my head and trying to sniffle back tears.

"Shit! Gone head just tell me so I'll know if I need to make a pit stop by y'all house on my way to the airport, 'cause I know his ass there!" she huffed, meaning every word. My bitch was a firecracker after years of being with a street nigga who couldn't keep his dick in his pants. More times than I could count, we'd had to ride down on her now husband, Tramel, and whatever hoe he was messing with at the time. That was why I'd always been so thankful for Deshawn. I'd have always chosen a straight-laced, working man over a cheating ass dopeboy...until now. Knowing that she was willing to drop everything and come to my rescue had the tears I'd been holding back coming down my face as I told her about Erica. I left out the threesome though, too ashamed to even say it out loud despite no one else being around.

Before I could get it all out, she exploded. "I can't believe his ass! How the fuck he been living off you all this time but got the nerve to cheat! What Nikki say? Broke niggas should never cheat! She was literally talking about his ass!"

"That's not what she said," I pointed out with a shake of my head, unable to stop the laughter from bubbling up in my throat.

Her breathing got heavier as I heard her moving around, packing a bag because she was indeed preparing to jump her ass on a plane right then and there.

"So! That's what she should've said! And he better hope I don't accidentally drive into that nice ass BMW on my way to the airport."

"We're too damn old to be fuckin' up niggas' cars and shit ,Vyn. I'll settle for a divorce and never seeing him again."

"Tuh! As long as niggas ain't too old to cheat on their wives, we ain't too old to tear up their shit! Matter fact, it's better when they're over thirty 'cause their shit more expensive!" She was on a roll and had me cracking the fuck up by now, even though I knew she wasn't trying to be funny. The elevator dinged as I reached the first floor, and I stepped out into the lively lobby and wasn't surprised at all to see so many people around at damn near three in the morning.

"Hold up, was that the elevator? Where yo' ass goin'? It's too late to be travelin' alone in a strange place girl, sex trafficking is real." She quickly got serious and I rolled my eyes again.

"I'm actually going back to my room. I was only getting some ice, mama," I lied sarcastically, already knowing that if I didn't she'd harass me until I returned to my room for real, and I really needed something to take the edge off and help me sleep.

"Mmhmm, talk all the shit you want, I'm just trying to look out, but don't worry, I'll be there in a few hours and we can go out to find you a new husband."

"And what about Tyrese?" I quizzed, talking about our friend and her business partner completely skipping right over the part about finding me a new husband. "Don't you think you should let him know you're randomly hopping on a flight to Miami?"

"Girl, fuck Tyrese! He'll be fine, he likes when I'm not there anyway so he can be gossiping and blasting that ratchet ass music." I had to laugh at that because it was definitely true. As wild and crazy as Sevyn was, she didn't play that shit in their salon, but every time she left Tyrese's ass in charge there was always a fight and some twerking going on. "Hey boo, let me call you right back, Tramel's calling," she interrupted my thoughts in a rush. Normally, I would've been irritated, but since I was about to make up an excuse to get off the phone anyway, I didn't put up a fuss.

"Okay, talk to you in a bit."

"Kk, bye."

I ended the call and scanned the lobby, noting the lights coming from a section off to the side and headed in that direction. By now the time was 2:45 and the bar looked to be empty, but as long as I could get me a stiff shot or two I'd be cool. I walked around the multiple velvet ropes that were blocking off the different entrances until I got to one where two buff ass men in suits stood. Unsure of whether I needed to show them ID or something, I stalled and looked between the two.

"Umm, do y'all card, or can I just go in?" The silence that followed had me feeling dumb as fuck, like they didn't even look in my direction, and my brows rose. Irritated by their rudeness, I went to walk in and they promptly stepped in my way, making me stumble backwards a little. "Um, excuse me?"

"The bar's closed," was the dry ass response I got as they both kept their eyes straight ahead. Flabbergasted, I looked around them, knowing damn well I saw a man sitting at the bar and a bartender inside when I walked up. My frown deepened seeing that the guy was indeed there and being served a drink while I was being denied by the Debo twins.

"No, it don't close for another ten minutes and it's clearly somebody inside still, so you need to move!" I was hoping I was loud enough that the guy and bartender heard me over the low music, but neither looked in our direction and I grew even more irritated. Sucking my teeth, I again tried to move past them, but they stood firmly, both rocking the same blank ass stare as before. I really wasn't trying to look like a whole drunk that would start a fight with security just for a taste of alcohol, but with everything I had going on, the very least I could have control over was being able to get a drink at the bar. "Oh, y'all muthafuckas must wanna get fired! Let me find out y'all ain't letting me in 'cause I'm black! Is it 'cause I'm black?" I shouted, unfazed by the attention I was drawing at this point.

"Ma'am, the bar is *closed* to the general public!" the bigger of the two grit, mugging me. Whatever else he was about to say was cut off by a loud whistle that snatched both their attention. Even my eyes shot to the man at the bar who still had his back turned.

"Let her in!" The timber of his voice sent a shiver down my spine. Almost immediately, the two guards moved aside, granting me entrance, but the whole display suddenly gave me pause. Noticing the way I switched up had the one who'd just yelled at me smirking as he nodded for me to go inside.

"Gone head, gangsta."

The sarcastic way he said it seemed like a challenge and despite my apprehension, I straightened my shoulders and brushed past him. Once I was inside, it seemed like a completely different world even though we were only separated from the outside by a few partitions. The low blue lights and classic R&B playing made the mood seem romantic, but at the same time the cool demeanor of the man in charge was off-putting to say the least. I took slow timid steps toward the circular bar, and he slowly turned around with a look I could only describe as annoyed plastered on his handsome face. Suddenly, my heart was pounding at just how handsome he was. His light skin was smooth and half covered by a full beard that only added to his ruggedness. He had thick brows that covered his deep-set, almond-colored eyes in a way that made him appear even angrier than he probably was. My nerves must have been evident, because his succulent lips spread and he nodded at the seat beside him.

"Take a seat," he said gruffly. The way it came out as more of a demand than a request had my ovaries in a frenzy, and I made up my mind right then that *he* was going to be my revenge on my husband, but first I had to change whatever bad impression he had of me. Taking a deep breath, I moved to do as he said, sliding onto the stool next to him. *Here goes nothing.*

Shai A'santi

Sexy. There was no other word to describe the woman that was suddenly in my space smelling like my mama's peach cobbler. The last thing I had been expecting when I heard her acting a fool with the guards was somebody that looked like *her* being the culprit. I'd been in Miami for almost a full twenty-four hours and every woman that approached me was Spanish, or racially ambiguous with a model-thin figure and a nasty attitude even though they'd been the ones coming on to me. I wasn't there for pussy though, especially when it was just as plentiful in my own damn city. Pussy being thrown at me was a regular occurrence, but I never indulged because I *loved* my woman, Kendra. Unfortunately, the bitch loved more than just me, and if I hadn't seen it with my own two eyes I probably wouldn't have believed it.

My cousin Zaakir was all too happy to show me the Instagram video with her hugged up on a nigga named Kyrie that she knew I didn't fuck with. A long-standing beef between his father and my sperm donor was the reason he was in a one-sided competition with me, when I couldn't give a fuck less about him. The only reason he'd probably even sniffed in Kendra's direction was because of me, much like everything else he did. He was a clown and she was unwittingly swept up in his circus. I had yet to even confront her about the shit, which was part of the reason why I was out of town. After making that nigga Kyrie a distant memory, I'd hopped on a plane so I wouldn't be tempted to send her ass out just like I'd done him. I was already in deep enough shit and was actively ignoring my uncle Casanova's calls along with my cousin, Zaakir's. By now I was sure they knew exactly what I'd done and were ready to chew me out, but I wasn't beat for any lectures or to face the consequences of my emotional ass actions.

"Sooo, you must be pretty important for them to reserve the bar just for you and keep the doors open past 3," shorty mused, snapping me out of my thoughts. The bartender, Rema, had already set a fruity looking drink down in front of her and was standing close by trying hard to control her irritation. Before I'd invited the beautiful woman inside, we'd been having a slightly flirtatious conversation where she was slyly throwing the pussy at me, and although I hadn't really taken the bait, I hadn't immediately denied her so she was probably hoping to wear me down. Unfortunately for her though, the beauty to the right of me had my attention now.

Shrugging, I focused on my half-empty glass of top shelf cognac and quickly tossed it back before answering modestly, "You could say that." The truth was, I was one of *the most important*, especially when every time I stopped through I spent thousands, and considering how much business I did in the city of Miami, I was there quite often. She nodded coolly, stirring her little straw around her glass, and I couldn't help being pleasantly surprised by how she didn't immediately begin asking me more questions about my status. Instead, she took a sip of her drink while I motioned to Rema to refill mine.

"What made you decide to let me join you?"

She looked up at me through her lashes and I let my eyes linger on her face before slowly lowering down her thick body. She had a sickening shape, almost like she'd gotten a BBL, but I knew with just a look there wasn't shit about her that was fake, and the thin shawl thing she had on did little to hide it. Bringing my attention back to her face, I saw the semblance of a smirk there, like she knew she had me mesmerized. The liquor had me returning the gesture with a shrug. "You seemed like you could use a drink too. What you got on your mind that brought you out this time of night?" I found myself asking. It was obvious she was dealing with some shit, and although I wasn't usually a nosey nigga, I couldn't help being intrigued by the curly haired, brown-skinned beauty.

That question had the smile slipping right from her face and her spine straightened as she polished off her drink.

"A lying, cheating ass nigga," Sshe grumbled bitterly and pushed her glass toward Rema. "Can I get another one and two shots of Patrón?"

What were the odds of us both ending up in the same bar for the same reason? I snorted unconsciously while she downed both her shots, releasing a low hiss after each one. "Well, he's a damn goofy for fumbling yo' beautiful ass."

She finally turned her head in my direction and her lips curved up into a slow smile. "You're damn right." Snickering, she extended her hand toward me. "I'm Zuri."

"Shai."

I swallowed her hand up in mine and immediately noted how soft it was, matching literally everything else about her, including her name. "Shai," she repeated slowly, and I could almost see her tossing it around in her head. The way it rolled off her tongue was sexy without even trying, and I wondered if it'd be just as alluring while I was fucking her mercilessly. "I like it. You don't seem like the shy type but somehow it suits you."

"You can thank my mama for that. Her ass was in love with the group when she got pregnant with me." I shook my head and chuckled at the thought and Zuri did the same once realization of who I was talking about set in.

"Oh wow, I didn't even make the connection but that just makes it even cuter."

"I'm a grown ass man love, ain't shit *cute* about me."

She giggled despite the deep frown on my face, and I knew she was beginning to feel the effects of the alcohol she'd consumed. I couldn't lie, either the liquor was hitting me too or her company had me forgetting all about the reason I was there trying to drown my sorrows in a bottle.

We spent the next hour drinking more, much to Rema's chagrin, and I found out more about Zuri. I was surprised to hear that trifling exes weren't the only thing we had in common. Like me, Zuri was from Chicago and was an only child. She worked as a mortgage loan officer at First American Bank, which was where I banked. I'd never had a reason to venture into her office since I already owned my home, but it was still crazy that we'd never crossed paths in all the years I'd been going to make deposits. The more I learned the more I wanted to know about her. She was like a breath of fresh air after being with Kendra, who only cared about my appearance and status. Being attached to me had her feeling like hood royalty and despite being a very successful entrepreneur, she was way more enamored with being a trophy wife. Had I noticed a few qualities of hers that I didn't like during our two-year relationship...yes, but I was sure there was some things she didn't like about me either. I thought that's how relationships were supposed to be though. Give and take. Compromise. Loving somebody beyond their faults and all that bullshit. At the age of thirty, I wasn't trying to be fucking different women and being suspicious of all of them like Zaakir's ass. I wanted something real and that's what I planned to get.

Zuri's hand on my thigh pulled me back into the present. Four of those fruity drinks and a couple shots had loosened her up completely. She'd been giggling and cracking jokes as we talked and got to know each other, but now she was looking at me with the most serious face she could muster.

"Shai, I want you to...fuck me."

Rema sucked her teeth from behind the bar and grumbled something, but a look from me silenced her and she went back to washing glasses like she should've been doing in the first place.

Turning back to Zuri, I lifted her hand and kissed it before setting it back on her own leg with a pat.

"You're drunk love, I'ma walk you back to your room." Her face fell and I instantly felt bad for hurting her feelings, but I wasn't going to take advantage of her either. As many drinks as we'd both had, she probably wouldn't even remember the shit anyway. Shaking off the rejection, she allowed me to help her to her feet. I locked arms with her so I had a more secure hold just in case she stumbled.

I ignored Rema asking if she could come up instead and continued out the door with Zuri in tow. As I passed, I let my security know that I was good from here before escorting her to the elevator. She stood silently, looking everywhere but at me as we waited for the car to reach us and once the doors slid open, I allowed her to step on first. She eased over to the far corner while I stopped to put our floors in.

"What floor?" I asked, drawing her attention from her manicured toes.

"Eight," her lips barely parted as she said. Nodding, I pressed the button for her floor and relaxed against the wall as we ascended. I could feel my phone vibrating in my pocket, and I pulled it out to see Zaakir calling for the hundredth time. Frowning, I hit the side button and returned it to my pocket, making a mental note to call his ass back the next day. By then I figured I'd be in a better mood to deal with the bullshit back home.

"I'm not drunk, you know." Zuri broke the silence that had fallen over us.

"Huh?" My thoughts had already shifted to going upstairs and smoking the exotic weed I'd gotten earlier, so I was lost on what she was even talking about.

"I *said*, I'm *not drunk*," she repeated, this time with her perfectly arched brows pushed together. Sighing, she let her gaze shift away from me like she was ashamed to say what came next. "I just...I just wanted to *feel wanted* for just being me, not because I did something for you or because somebody else was involved.

Just because I'm sexy, and smart, and witty...you know?" Her voice cracked and she quickly wiped her face, turning to try and stop me from seeing her cry. The elevator dinged indicating that we'd reached her floor, and she went to rush off. Before she could slip out though, I caught her hand, pulling her back silently. Confusion covered her face as I wrapped my arm around her, bringing her body against mine so she could feel the hardness I'd been trying to conceal since she'd offered herself up to me. Her dark eyes widened at the realization and she went to speak, but I covered her lips with mine, tasting the hint of pineapple that lingered from the drinks she'd consumed. Her lips were just as soft and succulent as they looked and I hungrily parted them with my tongue, deepening the kiss. Squeezing her ass, I groaned inwardly as my dick grew harder and fished my key out my pocket.

The sexy ass whimper she let out had me instantly regretting pulling away so that I could insert my key to get us to the penthouse. Her lids were low, and she kept her head tilted up toward me, anticipating my lips back on hers. No lie, she looked even sexier than she had when I first laid eyes on her, and I quickly gave her what she wanted this time, cupping her face softly. When we finally reached my floor, I backed away from her and entered the foyer, extending a hand back for her, which she timidly accepted. If feeling wanted was what she craved, then I was going to make sure I gave her the night of her life.

SHAI A'SANTI

Once we were far enough inside I guided her through the open layout until we reached the stairs for the second level, noting the look of awe that washed over her face as she took it all in. No lie, the Sorrento Penthouse was nice as fuck and whenever we came out to Miami it was reserved for us. The hefty price was probably the only reason it was even available to me for this impromptu trip.

"This is...nice," Zuri mused, trying unsuccessfully to sound nonchalant, and we shared a chuckle.

"Thanks." The five-room, five-bath suite with a full living area, dining room, and kitchen was nothing to turn your nose up at, and if that hadn't impressed her, the jacuzzi, pool, and terrace definitely took it up a notch. Reaching the master, I began emptying my pockets, before taking off my suit jacket and unbuttoning my shirt as she stood by taking in the breathtaking view.

"Should I undress or do you want to?" her voice trailed off, and I lifted my head to see her standing there awkwardly. She wasn't the same sultry and fiery woman from the bar but she also wasn't the vulnerable one from the elevator either. After that whole act that she'd put on downstairs and then opening up on the elevator, she was now full of uncertainty. Usually, I wasn't the type to help a woman out of her clothes, and not because I never wanted to, but because every woman I'd bedded had it in their mind that they'd seduce me. I'd gotten so used to the act that I'd come to expect it, but I could tell I was going to have to take a different approach with Zuri. I didn't mind though, because undressing her was going to be like unwrapping a present on Christmas. She fidgeted under my intense gaze, looking like she was about to run.

"Come here." The command had her mouth dropping open and she shivered unconsciously before doing what I said, as I removed one of the two condoms from my wallet. When she finally reached me, I pulled her thick frame into mine and she instinctively wrapped her arms around my neck. Sucking her lip into my mouth, I backed us into the bathroom, pulling away briefly to start the shower.

While the water ran, I trailed wet kisses down her neck and slid her shawl from her shoulders, pressing a kiss there too as it billowed to her feet. The thin straps of her bodysuit came next, and her breasts popped free. I let out a low groan seeing the heart-shaped nipple rings there, and I took my time giving each of them my attention, nibbling gently as she hissed and ran her fingers through my hair. Continuing down further, I dipped my tongue in her belly button and even lower past her freshly waxed pussy and her meaty thighs. Face to face with her glistening pussy lips, I looked up at her as I covered them with my mouth and snaked my tongue through her folds.

"Oh my..." Her knees buckled and I held the backs of her thighs to keep her steady.

"Keep your eyes open, love. I want you to watch me make yo' sexy ass cum." Panting, she let her eyes flutter open as her face contorted from the assault I was inflicting on her clit. She spread her thighs further apart and I slipped two fingers inside of her, stroking her g-spot until she cried out and soaked my hand with her juices.

"Ohhhh yesss! Right there, right there, don't stop!" Her grip on my hair tightened and she stiffened as she reached her climax and began shaking uncontrollably. I tried to lap up every drop of nectar that splashed out even as I continued working my digits in her center until she tried to push me away. "Waaaiit!" she begged, trying to wiggle out of my grip, but I only held her tighter, latching back onto her sensitive clit. I wasn't stopping until her legs felt like jelly and she blessed me with more of her sweet juices. A few seconds later, she did just that and just like before, I licked her as clean as I could. While she tried to recover, I finished helping her out of her clothes and shoes. Without the platforms she had dropped a couple more inches in height and was now just under my chin. I wasted no time sucking her tongue in my mouth so she could taste just how delicious she was. Her freaky ass moaned sexily and kissed me with an urgency that had precum oozing out my dick.

I quickly undressed and stepped inside the steamy hot shower, pulling Zuri right along with me. I already had it in my mind how I was about to fuck her up against the shower door but she flipped it on me, backing me into the wall. She slid down my body, grabbing ahold of my dick and quickly made it disappear. How she'd swallowed me whole had me growing harder in her mouth and I was already on the verge of exploding. I grabbed a handful of her thick hair, trying to get a handle on her as she sucked and slurped savagely like she had something to prove.

"God damn, baby," I groaned, tucking my lip between my teeth to keep me from sounding like a bitch. It had been a couple days since I busted a nut and it felt like Zuri was about to suck every drop out of me within minutes. Shorty had my toes balled up and I just knew if the head was that good then the pussy had to be spectacular. Unable to take it any longer, I tilted her head back and sloppily kissed her. The anticipation of sliding up in her walls had me pressing her up against the shower door as I struggled to open the condom and pull it on snuggly. I lifted her with ease, cuffing her legs in the crooks of my arms, and placed myself at her center, instantly feeling the heat there.

"Ooooo!"

"Fuuuuuck!"

We panted at the same time as soon as I eased my way inside of her. She was super tight and soaking wet, squeezing the life out of my dick and I was barely in there. I paused, cursing under my breath at how fucking good she felt. To distract myself, I sucked each of her small breasts into my mouth, making her whimper softly. I took my time easing in and out of her slowly, making sure to look into her eyes as I did. Without meaning to, Zuri made the sexiest fuck faces I'd ever seen and I couldn't stop looking at her.

"Shai, baby!" she whined, trying to close her eyes on me, but I quickly put an end to that.

"Open yo' eyes, I'm tryna see how good this dick feel to you, love." I grinned cockily when she did as she was told before dropping a quick kiss on her lips. "You gone wet me up again, baby?" I couldn't help asking, knowing that if I felt her squirting on my dick it'd probably bring me to my fucking knees, but not even caring.

"Oh my—yeeesss! Yessss! I'm bouta cum!"

"That's what I like to hear," I grunted, keeping my stroke steady even as I felt her walls begin to constrict, and her juices shot up between us, splashing my stomach. Her eyebrows drew together and her mouth widened. "Damn, you look so fuckin' sexy right now."

Aftershocks had her body shaking and she held onto my neck tightly. With my dick still buried inside her, I moved us over to the bench in the corner and sat down, letting her legs fall on either side of me.

"You good?" I tapped her thigh with a chuckle when she still hadn't lifted her head from my shoulder a few seconds later.

"Mmhmm," she hummed and sighed heavily. I bit back a laugh at how she'd asked me to fuck her and couldn't even handle it.

"Good, ride this dick like a good girl then," I told her, thrusting my hips so that she jolted up and back down, sending a tingling sensation through my body. The look of determination on her face when she sat upright had my dick jumping in anticipation, and when she began riding me like a real-life cowgirl, I knew exactly why. Planting her feet on the floor, she alternated between bouncing and grinding as she looked me in the eyes.

"Like this?" she wanted to know, licking my lips without missing a beat.

"Fuuuck yeah!"

I let my hands roam her wet body, showing extra attention to her plump ass while I sucked anywhere my mouth landed. Within minutes I could feel my dick swell and my balls grew tight. I held her tighter and pumped into her rapidly until I exploded, resting my head on her chest as I tried to catch my breath. My dick throbbed, still shooting out my seeds into the condom.

The water had lost some of its heat and I lifted Zuri to her feet so we could wash up before it turned cold. Tossing the condom in the trash, I handed Zuri a towel and the bottle of Dove soap, making her brows raise.

"Don't look at me like that, you know that shit moisturizing as hell." I laughed but I was dead serious. My mama had put me on a long time ago and it was mandatory that I kept it stocked.

"I ain't sayin' nothin'." She threw her hands up in surrender, laughing too.

We lathered our towels in silence and washed each other thoroughly just in time before the water turned ice cold. Wrapped up in the hotel's fluffy body towels, I carried her to the bed, ready to feel her again. I planned to never have her doubting how beautiful she was by the time I was finished, even if it took all night.

ZURI ROSS

The constant buzzing of my phone had me frowning with my eyes still closed. I hadn't felt like I was super drunk the night before, but now I was aching all over and my head was pounding way too hard to talk to anybody. Between the annoying buzzing and the sun burning through my lids, I was ready to curse somebody out. I blindly reached for my phone and opened one eye to screen the call just in case it was Deshawn's ass trying to reach me from an unknown number, but seeing my bestie's name I went ahead and answered, closing my eyes back as I did.

"He—ahem, hey bitch." My voice came out groggy and sounding mannish.

"Don't hey bitch me! What the fuck you doin'! I been calling yo' ass for the last forty-five minutes, bitch! Got me in this lobby lookin' like a hobo and bouta cuss Jessica's ass out!" Confusion washed over me before realization did and my eyes popped open. I'd forgotten all about her flying down. Springing up from the bed, I winced in pain from the throbbing in my head and the dull ache between my legs. *What the fuck!*

"Oh my god! I'm so sorry, I forgot!"

"Yeah, I know hoe, just tell me your room number so I can

come up, 'cause if this bitch keeps looking at me crazy it's gone be a problem down here!" she hollered before muffling the phone, but I could still distinctly hear her cursing somebody out. I quickly ran down my room number as I swung my feet out of bed and searched for the slippers I'd brought with me, only to find them nowhere in sight. Frowning, I looked around for my suitcase and again came up empty. My eyes landed on a pair of huge men's dress shoes and I finally took in my surroundings as the events of the previous night came flooding back. *I was still in Shai's room!*

The realization had my gaze shooting back to the empty bed, and I breathed a sigh of relief until it hit me that if he wasn't in bed then he was up somewhere. Groaning, I said a silent prayer that he'd run downstairs or left completely so I could sneak my hoe ass out, but that glimmer of hope quickly evaporated at the sight of his wallet on the dresser. No way he'd left without that! As if on cue, the sound of someone talking floated through the closed door and I panicked even more.

"Don't be doin' all that Zee, I'm not even about to slap this lily-white bitch for real. I'm already getting on the elevator now, I'll see you in a sec."

Unable to speak, I nodded like she could see me and hung up so I could think. The last thing I wanted was to face Shai again, but I also wasn't trying to let Sevyn's ass know I'd gone out and cheated on my husband, no matter what he did. She'd never let me forget it and she'd be trying to play matchmaker like I wasn't already married. I *had* to beat Sevyn to the room. Rushing into the bathroom, I found my clothes and hurriedly wiggled into them, then threw some water on my face and hair. I scrambled to find a spare toothbrush and when I realized that was taking too much time, I settled for squirting some toothpaste on my finger and doing a quick sweep of my mouth. I avoided looking at myself in the mirror because I knew I looked a whole damn mess despite the little effort I'd put in. Taking a deep breath, I snatched up my phone and shoes before making my way out of the room.

As I reached the stairs, it became clear that Shai wasn't the only one in the suite, and I groaned inwardly. Now, I had to do the walk of shame past two niggas! I mentally chastised myself for allowing Deshawn's bullshit to have me out fucking random men as I tiptoed down to the first level.

"Oh shit! Who do we have here, Shai?" I cringed despite knowing that I was going to be seen and shot a glance into the kitchen where Shai stood with a dark-skinned guy who was wearing a goofy ass grin.

"I, um...I'm Zuri." I felt dirty under his gaze and diverted my eyes back to Shai, who was looking at me curiously. He was shirtless, displaying his chiseled body, and my mind instantly flashed back to the night we'd had as he quickly licked his lips.

"*Zuri*," he repeated with an even bigger grin.

"Leave her alone, Zaakir. Don't mind my annoyin' ass cousin." Shai sent a stern look his way before settling his eyes on me. "You wanna stay for breakfast? I just ordered a bunch of shit since I didn't know what you'd want." He shrugged casually and although I got that jittery feeling inside from his thoughtfulness, I shook my head.

"I actually have to go. I'm late meeting someone." Something flashed over his face so quickly, I would've missed it if I wasn't paying attention.

"Oh damn, she curved you my boy!"

"Shut up, Zaakir," Shai grumbled, turning so he could set down his coffee mug.

"N-no, I really do have to—" I quickly tried to explain, but he cut me off while Zaakir gave me a doubtful look.

"It's cool love, I'll walk you out." The matter-of-fact tone he used had my mouth clamping shut. Now I was worried about hurting his feelings when my focus should've been getting my ass to my room. I had to remind myself that I was a married woman, and even if I did plan on divorcing Deshawn's ass there was no reason to believe that I'd ever see Shai again. He seemed like a cool guy, obviously wealthy and very attractive, but that was all the more reason why nothing more could come of the previous night. If a nigga like Deshawn that was just barely scratching the surface of success and was average looking had the ability to break my heart, then I knew a nigga like Shai could destroy it, and that was if he was even thinking about me. He was probably only being so nice because my big mouth ass had told him so much of my business during our drinking session. That thought had me filling with embarrassment as he rounded the corner, exuding book bae energy with his perfect body clad in only a pair of basketball shorts and some Nike slides. Even the man's feet were nice looking, like he went to the Chinese lady every two weeks like I did. My eyes traveled up his body, pausing at the huge print there. *God damn, I had that thing in my mouth!* My clit thumped as if trying to remind me that I certainly had, and I hurried to look away, meeting his intense gaze. He seemed amused, like he knew I was eye fucking him.

"You ready?" Something about the way he said it had a sexy undertone, or maybe it was just my ass being overly horny. Biting my lip, I nodded, mumbling a low yes that had a glimmer of a smirk playing at his lips as he stretched his arm out for me to go first.

"See you later, Zuri!" his cousin shouted out from behind us, and I could hear Shai grumble 'this nigga.' In only a few minutes of being around him, it was obvious that he was a jokester, but the way he'd said it was extremely matter of fact and not at all like he was trying to be funny. I couldn't really focus on that anyway though, because I was too busy trying to act naturally since I could literally *feel* Shai's eyes damn near caressing me. It was just as intense as if his hands were on me, and I shuddered as I made it to the elevator.

He came around me, invading my senses with his masculine scent and pressed the button, making the doors slide right open. "Thanks for last night." I hesitated to step on and looked up at him through my lashes.

"It was my pleasure, love," he said, pulling me into an embrace that had me weak in the knees, and then he put the cherry on top by pressing a soft kiss to my temple. The moment his hands were no longer on me, I hated the disconnect but I backed onto the elevator anyway. He stood there looking sexier than the night before as the doors shut separating us. Sighing, I fell against the wall feeling a mix of emotions. *Yeah, that man definitely had the power to crush me.*

I didn't have time to dwell on that fact though. Pressing the number for my floor, I tried to shake the whole encounter because feeling so bothered by that man wasn't supposed to be an issue. I was simply supposed to walk away feeling as if I had one up on my husband, but the effect Shai had on me plus the multiple orgasms was making that damn near impossible. My thoughts were so consumed that I didn't hear the bell alerting me that I made it to my floor. The doors opening and the sea of people bum rushing inside was what caught my attention. Sliding past them all, I stepped out into the hall and immediately saw Sevyn standing at my room door with a big ass pink rolling suitcase and a matching duffle sitting on top. She was already tapping her foot impatiently as she knocked on the door, so I knew her aggravating ass was mad.

"I'm right here! My bad, girl, I went to get some coffee," I said, rushing over while retrieving my key from my phone case. Her head snapped up in my direction and I guiltily slid past her to let us inside the room, intentionally avoiding her eyes.

"But I thought... Oooh, you sneaky hoe!" she gasped as we entered, stepping back so she could take me in. With narrowed eyes, she looked me over with her lips tooted.

"What are you talking about? I—"

"Nah uh, don't try that shit with me! I know what it looks like when a bitch sneakin' in! Yo' ass got some cutty last night!" Her voice dropped. "Messy hair, shifty eyes, mmhmm, I can smell it on you... Plus yo' clothes inside out."

"What!" I shrieked, checking to see how she could even tell, and she cackled like a psychopath.

"I knew it!"

"You didn't know shit," I grumbled, realizing that it wasn't anything wrong with my damn clothes. Rolling my eyes, I went to walk off and she skipped after me way too happily.

"It all makes sense now... You weren't on your way back to your room last night hoe, you were leaving! Not answering this morning when I called talking about you fell asleep, them ain't no pajamas, and I know yo' ass ain't get dressed that fast!!" She continued, "Then you weren't here when I just got here—"

"I went to get coffee, bitch." I plopped down on the foot of the bed, glaring at her, and was met with a 'yeah right' look from her.

"Where the coffee at then?"

I'd been so busy trying to lie, I hadn't thought it all the way through. Her grin widened the longer I took to answer and I fell backward, throwing my arm over my face with a groan. "Okaaay, you got me, damn!"

Squealing, Sevyn jumped her crazy ass on top of me, bouncing childishly. "I knew it, I knew it! I'm soooo proud of youuu!"

"Bitch, get yo' big ass off me!"

"Not until you give me allllll the details! What he look like? Where you meet him? Oh, did you make the first move or did he? How was it, better yet, how big was it?" she shot off question after question, not even giving me time to answer one before she was moving on to the next.

"Okay, I will as soon as you get off me. I'm already sore as fuck!" *Why did I say that shit?*

"Oh shit, if you're sore then I know it was good! Tell me more!" She made a big production of climbing off me, crossing her legs, and propping her chin on her fists like I was about to read her ass a book. I already knew she was going to do the most, and despite previously not wanting to tell her, I did want her opinion. Besides, if telling her about what happened with Shai kept me from having to talk about my husband then I was more than willing to give her all the juicy details.

Trying to keep Deshawn out of it as much as I could, I started with me going down to the bar and gave her a full recap. She interrupted occasionally, throwing in adlibs and dramatically asking questions until I got to the part where Shai and I said our goodbyes.

"Oh my gooood! Bitch, why didn't you stay and have breakfast with a side of dick?" She swooned, falling back on the bed with her hands on her heart, and I rolled my eyes before giving her a hard look.

"Well, for one, somebody had just shown up and was threatening to fight somebody in the lobby."

Frowning, she sat up abruptly. "First of all, I said I was bouta cuss that bitch out, and secondly, you could've just left me a key at the front desk if you knew you was going out hoeing—"

"I didn't know, it just happened." I side eyed her and she shrugged. "But anyway, now I can't stop thinking about him and wondering if there's something there." She was already shaking her head before I could finish.

"Nope! That's a big no-no, friend. You *never* fall for the one-night stand nigga." She huffed dramatically. "He seems sweet, but they all seem sweet at first and that's how they trap yo' ass and you end up married and alone while he one nights the next bitch." At this point, I didn't know if she was talking about my situation or hers, but before I could ask her specifics she was on her feet.

"We're going out tonight and I'ma show you how to do a one-night stand and before you try to argue, I brought you multiple fuck-him dresses, so go ahead and shower so we can take a nap and then get ready." Her phone went off and she sucked her teeth. "Gone head, this is just Tramel's aggy ass." She shooed me to the bathroom as she accepted the call, and I wasted no time removing myself from the room. Their conversations only went one of two ways: Either they were arguing over something stupid or he was trying to pin down where she was and what she was doing, and I wasn't trying to be around for it. Besides, I needed to shower and think because Sevyn hadn't really given me any real advice about my situation with Shai, and at least if I was alone I could reminisce and pretend like it was more than just a one-night stand, even if only for a little while.

SHAI A'SANTI

As soon as Zuri left and I returned to the kitchen, Zaakir was standing there with a big ass grin on his face. Instead of engaging with him though, I snatched up my mug and went to the sitting area, pissed that he'd even found me and even more so that he'd run Zuri off. Then again, she could've been running because she was feeling guilty for cheating on her goofy ass nigga, even though he didn't deserve her loyalty.

"Don't be mad at me 'cause ole girl curved you." He trailed behind me, dropping onto the couch while I opted for a chair.

"I ain't get curved, nigga." The growl in my voice only had his lame ass grinning harder and I just knew his face was hurting from stretching so much.

"That ain't what it looked like! You supposed to be tryna get over Kendra and yo' ass out here ordering breakfast and calling bitches 'love'!" he scoffed, shaking his head.

"Don't call her a bitch!"

Making some exaggerated noise, he tossed his hands up, looking at me in pity. "Nigga, you don't even *know* her ass and you caping already? Yo, you the quickest fallin' in love ass muhfucka I ever met! Wait 'til I tell my old man this shit. How the fuck you fall in love while you're laying low for killin' a nigga that was fuckin' the last girl you loved?" he asked, even though I knew he wasn't really expecting an answer.

"I gotta be in love to tell you not to call her out her name?"

"Yep, 'cause you don't know her ass so it shouldn't matter what the fuck I call her." The way he was looking at me said he fully believed everything he was saying, and I couldn't do shit but shake my head. My uncle, who had raised Zaakir on his own with the help of my mama, had really fucked his ass up. He'd be the first to tell anybody that Zaakir's mama was his first and only love. She'd died giving birth and according to my mama, he hadn't been the same since. For as long as I could remember, my uncle Casa had been a ladies' man, jumping from woman to woman, not giving a fuck who's heart he broke, and obviously the trait had been passed down to his only son.

"That's why hoes be playin' yo' ass the way they do, 'cause you're too lovey dovey, that's that light-skinned shit," he continued while I drank my coffee and tried to tune him out. "You gotta be mean to women, they like that shit. The meaner you are the more they like you—what?"

His eyebrows shot up when he saw the look I was giving him. It was hard to believe that the nigga was only a few months younger than me with the logic that came out of his mouth.

"I ain't fuckin' with you and that schoolyard ass logic."

"School yard? Nigga, this is facts, it may have started at recess but it's still how shit goes. These hoes still same, they just traded out barrettes for bundles and lip gloss for makeup and lash extensions." He shrugged and I damn near spit my coffee all over.

"Yo, you hell man."

"Naw, I'm real, you're the one tryna live out a Disney princess movie. It's a good thing I came so I can put you up on game. Help you live a little before my pops kill yo' ass. You know that nigga Kyrie daddy ain't waste no time accusing you," he said matter of factly, and I released an unbothered snort. I didn't really give a fuck what KG thought he knew, I'd more than covered my tracks. He was lucky I'd even left his ass a body to bury, but if he began making too much noise he was going to end up in the ground right next to him.

"Fuck KG! He ain't gone do shit." Unlike when we were talking about women, Zaakir's face was dead serious. My cousin played about a lot of shit but a possible threat wasn't one of them.

"You know we can't really bank on that though. Casa already thinking we gone have to have a talk with him." I knew exactly what he was hinting at and I nodded. "You know he ready to have a talk with Kendra's ass too for starting all this shit?" he added, and I sent a chilling look his way.

"Nigga, what!"

"Look at you, bouta have a heart attack. Ain't nobody bouta touch that girl, man." Shaking his head, he climbed to his feet. "You going out sad, bro. It should be fuck that bitch but yo' ass ready to go to war over her funny lookin' ass."

"I ain't—"

"Yeah the fuck you did, but it's cool. Super cuz here to show you how to get over a bitch. Shit, I might can get you a threesome if you play yo' cards right." He'd gone straight from business to pussy just that fast. I was glad the food came right then to distract him from the conversation. While he went to fix him a plate I went upstairs to lay down for a while since I hadn't gotten much sleep fucking around with Zuri. If it hadn't been for Zaakir's ass popping up, I'd probably have been knee deep in her pussy right then. It was cool though, because I'd make sure I ran into her again before heading back to Chicago. Heading into the master bedroom, I snatched up my phone and looked at the messy ass bed, reminiscing about how sweet and wet her pussy was. We'd run through both the condoms I'd had and then had to call the desk for more. I'd never had pussy so good that I couldn't get enough until I fucked Zuri, and now I was addicted. Looking at the bed one last time, I couldn't help but smirk thinking about how I was going to get her back in that motherfucker as soon as I could, before calling housekeeping and heading to the next room to sleep.

I'd woken up late in the afternoon, well rested and ready to find Zuri, but Zaakir was glued to my hip. He'd virtually crashed my getaway and inserted himself in my plans. First, the nigga wanted to go shopping since he hadn't brought any luggage and claimed that my shit wasn't his style, which just meant that his ass wasn't trying to wear another nigga's clothes, even if it was his cousin's. That ended up taking all day because he was like a woman when he shopped, knowing damn well he wasn't wearing none of that Miami Vice shit back home.

Every time I tried to creep the fuck off on his ass, he'd come up with an excuse to stay with me, so I knew either Casa had told him to keep an eye on me or he thought he needed to make sure I wasn't sulking over Kendra. He didn't have to worry about that though, because I was too busy thinking about Zuri.

I'd been able to slip Jessica at the front desk a couple bills to tell me if she'd left the hotel or not, but that was all she was willing to tell me without jeopardizing her job. Even though I was pissed about my influence not allowing me *everything* I wanted, I let her make it. All I really needed to know was that she was still there and I could work with that.

Now we were back in the room and I was waiting for Zaakir to finish getting dressed. He wanted to hit up Club Liv so he could put me up on game like he said. At my age, drinking two nights in a row wasn't something I really felt like doing, and I damn sure didn't want to be in a loud ass club, but I wasn't going to let him go alone. My cousin's mouth was always reckless and there was a big chance that he'd get into some shit if I wasn't there, but I was hoping he just found a woman to occupy his damn time so I could find Zuri. I was feeling like a feign and thoughts of Kendra were long gone like she never existed.

"What the fuck is you wearin'? You dressed like we bouta go to a business meeting!" Zaakir entered the living area with his nose turned up. Raising a brow, I looked down at the white Prada button up, black Prada slacks and matching loafers with the gold emblem. I thought I looked fine, but of course Zaakir's flashy ass wouldn't think so.

"You talkin' 'bout me when you look like you bouta take yo' kids to the beach. All yo' ass missin' is a bucket." I frowned, looking over his clothes. His style was completely different from mine; that much was evident from the blue and white-printed beach waves shirt and matching shorts. The Air Maxes on his feet matched the colors perfectly and he was shining from his ears, neck, wrists, and even his ankle. I hadn't even noticed the bucket hat and blue-lense shades he was holding until he stopped in the mirror and added them to complete his look.

"Naw, *this* how the fuck you s'posed to dress when you in Miami on vacation! It's a damn shame at yo' big age I gotta school you on bitches *and* what the fuck to wear, but that's what I'm here for, besides to make sure yo' ass don't slit yo' wrists over Kendra's hoe ass." he grumbled the last part, but I heard him loud and clear. I'd already figured that shit out.

"Guess yo' ass wasted a trip then, 'cause I ain't thinkin' 'bout her ass."

"Yeah, 'cause now you got Zuri on the brain." He looked at me in the mirror over the rim of his glasses. "Mmhmm, you ain't slick, nigga. I know yo' ass been stalkin', goin' around tryna get info on her thick ass. Jessica already told me after she sucked my dick earlier." I wasn't even surprised by his antics at this point and if anything, I wished I'd known he was busting her down because I probably would've gotten better results.

"I ain't stalkin' shit nigga, I was just tryna see if she was still here—"

"That's literally the definition of stalkin' but don't trip, it's gone be plenty pussy at the club to take yo' mind off her ass." While he spoke, he unbuttoned his shirt, revealing a white wifebeater underneath, and nodded before turning around and checking the time on his iced-out Patek. Come on, it should be packed by now," he said, rubbing his hands together as he headed to the door. As bad as I wanted to not be around a bunch of drunk people, I got up from the couch, checking my vibrating phone as I did. I'd blocked Kendra, but every so often she'd call from a random ass number so I'd have to block those too. It was beginning to become a chore though, and I knew eventually I'd have to answer, but now wasn't the time.

We made it to Liv a short time later and I wasn't even surprised by the long ass line of people waiting to get in. A lot of them were out of towners like me and Zaakir, so they were accepting the whole spiel about the club being at capacity when I knew damn well it wasn't, which was why we were able to walk right in. We didn't even have to identify ourselves and they had a voluptuous bottle girl with bundles down her back escorting us to one of the view tables that was stocked with bottles on top of bottles.

Zaakir wasted no time getting the girl's number before snatching up two bottles of Ace and drinking from them both like this was the early 2000s, while I opted to pour myself a glass of Macallan 12. I was already irritated because he hadn't splurged on a skybox, but I knew that was only because he wanted to mingle, with his friendly ass. I'd resigned myself to watching him act a drunk ass fool before finding a girl to entertain. Sitting back, I rested my arms along the back of the couch and bobbed my head to the Future song they were playing as I glanced over the crowd below. Almost immediately, something bright orange amongst the sea of people caught my eye. Her back was to me but I recognized that ass anywhere, and I smirked. The night had just gotten a whole lot more interesting.

SEVYN ELLIS

The vibe in the club was already giving me life as me and Zuri sat down at the table I'd booked for us. I rolled my eyes when I caught her pulling at the dress I'd picked out for her and tapped her hand like she was a small child. "Stop doing that, you look great." And I wasn't lying. The bright color looked amazing against her brown skin and it perfectly accentuated her shape by cinching in all the right places. I'd made sure not to pick her prudish ass nothing that was too revealing, but she was focused on the cleavage area and the cut out underneath. It was modest compared to what I was wearing, but she obviously didn't think so.

"Thanks, but I'd look better if I didn't have my titties hanging all out." She sucked her teeth, still trying to adjust her dress.

"You barely got any titties to be falling out in the first place, so don't even worry about it." Her mouth fell open like she was shocked, even though she knew it was true. My girl was in a whole B-cup, which made it almost impossible to find anything she could wear with a plunging neckline, and she was whining about the little piece that was open.

"Oooh, don't play with me! My mama told me anything more

than a mouthful is a waste anyway!" she clapped back, making me bust out laughing.

"Miss Zora ass funny as hell," I said, shaking my head. Zuri's mama was always saying something crazy, and I often wished I had a mom like her instead of having spent my childhood bouncing around from house to house before being sent to a group home until I was eighteen. From what I'd been told, there wasn't much information on my mama except that she was young and couldn't afford to take care of me. Although I'd long since let go of the hope I would find her, occasionally I'd get that feeling when I was around Miss Zora. Shaking off my depressing ass thoughts, I reached for one of the bottles of Patrón I'd purchased for us and hurried to pour her a shot. When I had the tiny glass filled to the rim, I slid it over to Zuri, but she was already shaking her head.

"No, Patrón is part of the reason I was face down, ass up with a nigga I don't know from Adam." I tried to hide my smile at the mention of her getting her back blown out but I couldn't help being proud. She still hadn't gone into details about what Deshawn had done to hurt her this time, but whatever it was, I was glad that she'd gone and got some revenge dick on his ass. Ever since I'd met that nigga, I didn't like him. It didn't matter how she tried to dress him up, talking about his accomplishments and education, I still thought he was a bum and he'd been proving me right from day one. In my opinion, he deserved every bit of karma that came his way and I was going to make sure she had the time of her life before she went back to deal with him.

"Oh, well then, in that case, drink up boo!" I egged her on, pushing the drink even closer. If I had anything to do with it, she was going to be like that again and if she needed a few drinks to loosen up, then so be it. Pouting, she lifted her glass and I twerked in my seat before filling my own. "To being face down ass up!" I toasted, clinking our glasses together. She didn't repeat it like she was supposed to, but she *did* down the shot, wincing as she swallowed. I was already refilling our glasses when "Throw Sum Mo" by Rae Sremmurd and Nicki Minaj came on.

"Awww, this used to be my shit!" Zuri gushed, bouncing in her seat, and I slid her glass back her way. She quickly drank it and once I did the same, I pulled her to her feet and we rapped along, shaking our asses. We got even more amped when the ladies at the table next to us started hyping us up. I locked eyes with a nigga over by the bar and winked at him as I made my ass cheeks bounce like I was a stripper. The sheer black one piece I was wearing left very little to the imagination and when his gaze lowered, so did mine. His print was clearly visible in the salmon-colored pants he wore, and I bit my lip, clocking him as the potential nigga I'd be going home with that night.

It had been a long ass six months since I'd let my side nigga go after he refused to accept the fact that I wasn't leaving my husband for him. I'd met Justin about three years into my husband Tramel's sentence while I was still trying to be a ride or die. He was the first nigga whose number I'd accepted since Tramel got hit with a twenty-year bid, and honestly, at the time, I didn't know what I'd planned to do with it. Like I said, I was trying to be the type of woman that stood by her man and all that, but those lonely ass nights were beginning to take a toll on me. I'd gotten used to sleeping next to somebody, getting affection, attention, and being spoiled and all that romantic ass couple shit. Tramel wasn't perfect and there'd been times that I had to go upside him and a hoe's head for playing with me, but he always came home and he always let me know I was the number one woman in his life. So, going three years alone and knowing I had seventeen more to go was beginning to take a toll on me. I figured I'd be the same dutiful wife to Tramel because honestly, he was still giving me financial support and as much emotional support as he could from behind bars, and I'd just have Justin for the physical. That's what I'd been thinking anyway, but it wasn't long before his ass was asking for more of me than I could give him. Yes, I cared about him, but I wasn't dumb enough to believe our relationship could go any further than what it was. For one, Justin owned a mechanic shop and while he made good money, it wasn't near enough to actually support my lifestyle if I were to leave my husband. And for two, him being a blue-collar nigga wasn't going to benefit either of us once Tramel found out. There was no way he was going to let me ride off into the sunset with the next nigga, prison sentence or not. I was a lot of things but I wasn't a fool, and I definitely didn't have a death wish, so leaving him wasn't an option and since Justin wouldn't accept that, I had to let him go.

Since then, I had been making the best of the situation, overusing my toys and fingers and watching the shit out of Porn Hub, but it was only so much any of those could do. I needed the real thing and this trip to Miami was the perfect opportunity to get some unattached dick and go on about my business.

Zuri and I had just sat back down after dancing through three songs when a bottle girl walked over with a ten-thousand-dollar bottle of champagne, and I stopped her ass before she could sit it down. My salon was doing great, especially with the added help of Tramel's business, so I had money, but not waste a bag on liquor in the club money. "Oh no, we didn't order that."

"This is compliments of the gentleman over there." She smiled, still setting it on the table while me and Zuri followed her finger to a section above us where a fine ass man sat looking down at us. When he noticed us looking, he lifted the glass of brown liquor he was drinking with a slight smirk.

"Ohhh shit! That's him!" Zuri's dramatic ass hissed, turning to me with wide eyes.

"Wait, *that's* the nigga from last night?" I asked for clarification. I could already tell that he was rich, he was obviously attractive, and she'd told me how he'd fucked her into oblivion so I knew he was packing. My girl had definitely done her big one and I was even more proud than I'd been when she'd first told me. She tried to discreetly cover her face as she nodded, and I elbowed her with a smile. "Damn bitch, he look good as fuck! And he got that bag! I see why you were acting all thirsty this morning. Fuck everything I said, you definitely need to be fucking *him* again."

"Really Sev?"

"Yes, *really*! Now smile and wave so he knows you appreciate the drink," I told her and was about to do so myself, but he was already on his way. "Oooh, he's coming over!"

"What!" The way her eyes bucked almost sent me into a fit of laughter. I could see why she was so pressed. The man she'd unwittingly given the goods up to was definitely the type of man that could take a bitch away from her husband. Already he had put Deshawn to shame and I hadn't even met him yet. He moved through the crowed club with the confidence that only a young, fine ass, rich nigga could possess while I clocked that he had to be in the streets. I was willing to bet Zuri's green ass didn't know that though and I hoped it didn't give her second thoughts when she found out. "Oh my god, what should I do?" she panicked, trying hard to avoid looking in his direction.

"First of all...relax. You look good as fuck in that dress, your hair is laid, and your face is beat to death. Plus, you can tell by the way his ass looking at you that he's on yo' ass, so it ain't shit for you to do but let him take you back to his room and wear that pussy out." Before she could respond he was already at our table and she couldn't even control the way her body responded to his proximity. It was so cute I almost blushed.

"It's nice seeing you again, love." The way he looked at her was too intimate for him to have just met her the night before, and I narrowed my eyes at her sneaky ass. She definitely had some explaining to do, but I was going to let her make it for now.

"It's good to see you too," she simpered, gazing up at him through the luscious falsies I'd put on her. "Uhh, this is my friend Sevyn, the one I was late meeting." As if just realizing that I was there, he tore his eyes away from Zuri and set them on me, smiling as he extended a hand.

"My bad, how you doin', friend? I'm Shai."

Smirking, I slipped my hand in his. "I'm good, thanks for the bottle by the way." He nodded, seemingly done with the conversation as he put his attention back on Zuri, going to take a seat next to her. As soon as he sat down, he was whispering in her ear and she was eating that shit up with a huge smile. I couldn't help feeling like a third wheel as I fixed me another drink and scanned the room. Zuri had found her something to get into and I needed to do the same.

Although the club was jam packed, the pickings were slim. Even the nigga I'd locked eyes with before was now booed up, and I frowned slightly as I downed a shot then quickly poured another.

"Ohhh, this where yo' ass dipped off to. I should've known... Heeeeeey Zuri!" Some nigga appeared clutching a bottle of Ace. Since he was looming over me, I took the time to look him over and I was pleased with what I saw. He was tall and chocolate just like I liked my niggas. The tan, blue-lined bucket hat he wore was low over his eyes, but I could still see that they were red and damn near slits. His goatee was freshly trimmed and I knew his hair was as well without even getting a good look. Diamonds shined from his ears, neck, and wrists, blinding me, and I unconsciously nodded in approval. Grinning sneakily, he eyed the couple who both seemed irritated by his presence, before shifting over to me.

"Hey Zaakir," Zuri said dryly as he took a seat and slid closer to me with an arm stretched across the back of the couch.

"This the friend you had to go meet?" he was asking her, but his eyes were still on me, taking in my shapely figure and licking his lips. "You gone introduce me?"

Lifting an amused brow, I leaned just a little closer, loving the scent of his cologne. "I can introduce myself, thank you."

"Oh word, what's yo' name then, *friend*?" he questioned with a playful smirk, putting extra emphasis on the word.

"I'm Sevyn... and you are?"

"Zaakir, I'm that nigga's cousin." He nodded toward Shai and I almost did a double take. It was hard to believe the two were related just from how different they were, but I opted not to mention that.

"Well, I guess since your cousin stole my bestie, that means you're keeping me company?" I flirted shamelessly, staking my claim on him for the night. I knew his type and he was the kind of nigga that was going to blow my back out and not care whether he ever saw me again, and that was exactly what I needed. Licking his lips, he flashed his teeth, showing just how white and straight they were.

"Oh hell yeah, I can definitely do that." He nodded and my smile widened. *I was going to enjoy this.*

ZAAKIR A'SANTI

As soon as I laid eyes on Zuri's homegirl, I knew I was going to shoot my shot, but her sexy ass beat me to the punch. Surprisingly, I liked that even though I usually hated when a bitch came on too strong. I was a nigga with money, plus I was fine as hell, so almost every day a hoe was throwing the pussy at me, but I was a man at the end of the day and I liked doing the chasing. Sevyn wasn't like anybody I'd come across though. She wasn't falling all over herself to get and hold my attention. In fact, I got the feeling that she'd easily move on to the next nigga if I changed my mind about kicking it with her that night. That was some sexy ass shit and besides her stacked frame and pretty face, it just made me want to fuck her more.

"So, y'all out here on vacation?" I found myself asking once we'd all relocated to our section. Normally, I'd have cut straight to the chase and already been trying to fuck her in the bathroom, but her nonchalance was...intriguing and had me wanting to know more about her secretive ass. She hadn't told me shit about herself outside of her name since I'd sat down and that wasn't some shit I was used to. Usually, females wouldn't shut the fuck up talking about themselves; where they went to school, what they did for a living, their interests. They thought that any of that shit would hold my interest and it never did, but somehow holding back all this information had me...interested.

She poured herself a shot and quickly threw it back before answering, "Uh, yeah something like that." She shrugged. "Are y'all?"

Realizing that her ass was intentionally trying to be vague, I did the same copying her. "Something like that." Her lips spread into the hint of a smirk before the beginning of Doja Cat's latest song came on and she stood up, swaying her fat ass as she rapped along. She wasn't even in my face but it felt like she was giving me a private dance with the way she was moving, hypnotizing me.

She did the same thing through two more songs, even getting Zuri to join her. Shai's possessive ass wasn't even enjoying the show. He was too busy mugging any nigga he caught looking in her direction, and there were plenty of them. No doubt they were some of the baddest bitches in the spot and since the club would be closing soon, those niggas were looking for something to lay up with.

When Sevyn decided to sit her ass back down, I wasted no time slipping my arm around her slim waist. "You comin' back to the room with me." It was more of an assessment than a question since I already knew the answer despite her ass playing hard to get.

"Only if you make it worth my while," she quipped with a wink, and I licked my lips.

"Oh fa sho." I gave her plump ass a squeeze. "I'ma fuck the shit out you and eat yo' pussy 'til you cryin'," I promised, like we weren't in a room full of people. I definitely didn't go around eating just anybody's pussy, but something in me needed to break Sevyn's ass down and I knew some tongue action was going to do the trick. Her eyelids lowered and she tucked her lip between her teeth sexily. I was damn sure ready to go and shot a look over to my cousin to see if he was too. They had already called for the last call so everybody was either trying to head to the bar or leave out and I wanted to beat the rush. Shai was a few steps ahead of me, helping Zuri to her feet. Once I saw that I did the same, standing and pulling Sevyn up with me. She hadn't seemed like it before but now that she was on her feet, it was obvious she was tipsy as fuck. Even with my help she stumbled a little and busted up laughing.

"Sevyn, you good girl?" Zuri called out.

"Yeeeesss!" her crazy ass answered, turning around so that her ass was pressed up against me, twerking with her tongue out. "Just bouta get me some diiiiick!"

"Yooo, chill out," I urged, wrapping my arm around her waist. She was showing the fuck out and while I usually wouldn't have given a damn, I felt some type of way about her treating me like a piece of meat.

"Okay—"

Snickering, she leaned into me and I shook my head in Shai's direction. After a bottle and a half of Ace plus the other shit I was drinking, the room was already spinning and I wasn't trying to have us both on the floor.

Thankfully we made it back to the hotel without incident. The whole elevator ride up, Sevyn was humming some shit that sounded familiar as hell but I didn't know where I'd heard it. The shit had her and Zuri both cracking up laughing while I racked my brain trying to figure out what it was, because it obviously meant something.

By the time we made it to the penthouse though, I'd given up, too drunk to be trying to guess riddles and shit. As soon as the doors slid open, Shai and Zuri stepped off and I waited a beat to get my bearings. It seemed like the more time passed the more drunk I felt. Sevyn took it upon herself to pull me from the back wall like her ass knew where she was going.

"Ooooh, this is niiiiiiice!" she said excitedly, and her loud ass voice bounced off the walls as she moved through the open area. She was about to head in the opposite direction of the stairs, but I yanked her back.

"We upstairs. I'm tryna beat that pussy up on a king-sized bed, baby."

The way she switched up the stairs I would've never thought she was just falling all over herself twenty minutes before. I followed closely behind her, unable to help letting my hands attach themselves to her waist. When we reached the landing, I guided her to the room I always stayed in and shut the door behind us. Sevyn immediately spun around, pressing me up against it and molding her body into mine.

She wasted no time capturing my lips with hers and slipping her tongue inside with a moan as she reached for my waist. "Damn, hold up." My face balled up as she pulled away so she could see since she was struggling with the drawstring.

She smirked triumphantly when she finally got it. "Nope." She quickly loosened them and pecked my lips before dropping to her knees.

"Aye man—" I went to pull her ass up because at this point I felt like she was taking the dick, but any objection I might've had got cut off the second she swallowed my shit whole. She didn't gag or make a sound besides moaning as she slid my ten inches down her throat with ease. Amazed, I watched as she gobbled it up then pulled it out, slapping her face like she didn't give a damn about the fucking up her makeup. "Ohhh, you a nasty bitch, huh?" I grunted, grabbing a handful of the bundles in her head. She was still rubbing my wet ass dick across her face, but she stopped long enough to nod, looking up at me innocently, and my knees buckled. *God damn!*

Once she'd thoroughly saturated her face she went right back to work. She was sucking me up like she loved a nigga, without even using her hands. She was sucking my dick so good I wanted to fuck her up, wondering who'd shown her how to do whatever she was doing that had my toes curling in my sneakers. I bit back a groan as I grew harder, stretching her mouth even more, and instead of easing up this crazy ass girl clutched the backs of my legs, pulling me in further. "Fuuuuck! I'm bouta nut all in that dirty ass mouth and you better catch every drop, bitch!" I had my chin tucked into my chest as I watched her, feeling my nut coming, but the second she stretched her tongue out and licked the area behind my balls, I exploded. My eyebrows bunched as I tried to control the way my body was jerking while it felt like I released buckets of cum down her throat, and she just continued swallowing until I finished.

I was still leaned up against the door trying to recover when she stood to her feet, clutching my still semihard dick tightly.

"Now give me that dick you promised," she demanded, burying her face in my neck as she stroked my dick back to life. I wanted to tell her ass to wait a minute while I got myself together and worked through the shit I was suddenly feeling, but I didn't want to sound like a bitch. I'd told her I was going to fuck the shit out of her and that's exactly what I was going to do, especially now since she had just showed the fuck out.

Tossing my hat across the room, I stripped out of the rest of my clothes, finding her lips as I walked her backwards to the bed. I helped her out of the one piece she had on and her body was even more amazing with nothing covering it. Everything she had to offer was on display since she was braless and her fat ass pussy lips were damn near busting out of the thin piece of fabric between her legs. "You was on some real slutty shit tonight, huh? Get on the bed, ass up," I ordered.

Like a true freak, she did so, stretching feline like with her knees spread far apart. Her ass and pussy quickly ate up her thong so I could clearly see her wetness in the moonlight, and I had to grab my dick because it was throbbing so hard, just yearning to slide up in her. Smacking her ass cheeks, I watched them jiggle before snatching the thin fabric off her and sniffing it. I could already smell her essence as soon as she'd spread her legs but I just needed to be sure before I committed to the nasty shit I was about to do to her.

"God damn that pussy leakin'. You got this wet just from suckin' my dick?" I mused, moving close enough that she could for sure feel my breath on her. She was so turned on that she was trying to toot that ass back and force it in my face.

"Yeeeeesss!"

I ran my finger down her slit and stuck it in my mouth, making a loud noise so she knew I'd tasted her, and fuck, it was just as good as it looked. Unable to hold back any longer, I covered her pussy lips with my mouth, flicking the tip of my tongue against her clit.

"Oooooh shit!" I'd barely done anything and her nasty ass was already quivering, but that just had me going harder. I sucked Sevyn's pussy until she came two more times and was running away. Even then I pinned her little ass to the bed and continued to assault her with my tongue. I had a point to prove and I wasn't going to stop until she was begging. Sucking her last orgasm out of her, I sat up with a satisfied smirk and wiped my mouth. Her sexual appetite was strong though because she recovered almost immediately, already raising her hips back up as she reached for me. Moving away, I went to the nightstand and was happy to see the box of condoms I'd requested right there. I pulled one out and proceeded to sheath my dick while Sevyn followed me with hungry eyes.

"You want this?" I questioned, making her eyes drop to my manhood that was stretched out before me. Nodding, she never lifted her head from the mattress. I took my time walking back behind her and climbed onto the bed as well, just barely letting the tip touch her center. "What you want me to do with it?"

"Slut me out," she said lowly, surprising me again. I was still teasing her with the head of my dick, but that had me trying to slip inside of her. Sevyn was so tight, I had to put in work just to get halfway there. With how tight she was squeezing me and her moaning out my name, I had to pause every so often so I wouldn't bust. "Zaakir, *please.*"

I was taking a pause but she threw her ass back, forcing me the rest of the way inside, and a nigga was in heaven. Even with the rubber on I felt every muscle in her pussy pulling me deeper.

"Fuuuck, throw that shit back then, Sevyn." I held her waist firmly while she went wild, slamming herself into me in a steady rhythm. All that could be heard was the sound of our skin slapping and her low moans. I knew damn well Shai and Zuri could hear her loud ass but I was definitely about to have her screaming. Flipping her over so that she was on her back, I pulled her to the edge of the bed. With one leg wrapped around my waist, I pinned the other one down by her head and slammed into her. She looked so fucking good with her red lipstick smeared and her eyes rolling into the back of her head.

"Baaaaby, you feel so good!" Leaning forward, I kissed her sloppily, sucking her chin and then each of her juicy titties. "Oooouu! I'm bouta—fuuuck!" She tightened even more and held on to me as another orgasm tore through her body. Smirking cockily, I stood at the foot of the bed and bent her knees so I could see just how creamy her pussy looked. Sevyn literally had my dick completely coated, and I knew right then I wasn't going to last much longer. Leaning over her once again, I laid stomach to stomach with her, squeezing her neck lightly as I picked up my pace.

"I'm bouta bust!" I groaned, feeling my face tightening as I choked her harder. "Fuuuuck, pull that nut up out me, baby!" As if following my command, she clenched her pussy around me and a few seconds later I was cumming hard as fuck. My dick continued to pulse as I fell on top of he,r filling the condom. She rubbed my back softly while I laid on her chest trying to catch my breath. It wasn't long before we were right back at it again, fucking from the bed to the shower and back before falling asleep spent.

I woke up with Sevyn's body wrapped around me and although I didn't want to move, the nagging ass sound of a cellphone going off was keeping me from going back to sleep. Knowing I'd put my shit on DND, I knew it had to be hers. She was peacefully snoring as I tossed the covers back and went in search of her shit. I found it sticking out of her bag, the vibration having knocked the whole thing over. Frowning, I snatched everything up just as the phone stopped ringing. As soon as it stopped it was ringing again, and I got the shock of my life seeing the word Hubby with a heart emoji behind it. My eyes shot over to where she was sleeping peacefully in bed and I had to resist the urge to go wake her hoe ass up. No wonder her hoe ass had been so nonchalant talking to me. *Her ass had a nigga!* The latest call had gone to voicemail and I hurried to block the number. I'd already realized that the reason I was so mad was because of the jealousy flowing through me. That wasn't an emotion I was used to, but knowing that Sevyn was already being claimed had my ass greener than a motherfucker and even worse, there wasn't shit I could do about it because her baldheaded ass was only supposed to be a one-night stand. *Fuck!*

ZURI ROSS

I sighed at the sight of Deshawn's truck as I pulled into driveway and instantly lost the good mood I was in. After spending a few days in Miami with Shai getting catered to and receiving multiple orgasms, the last thing I wanted to do was return home to the nonsense my husband had going on.

Before I could even get out of the girl's car good he was coming down the walkway with his face balled up. "Where the fuck have you been Zuri! I've been worried sick! The least you could've done is answered my calls and not blocked me!" he shouted like I was his child and not his damn wife. My cheeks warmed at him putting our business out there in front of a perfect stranger, but he didn't seem bothered at all.

"Please get the fuck out my face, Deshawn! You wasn't worried about me when you was fucking Erica on our vacation, so don't be worried now!" The driver popped the trunk as I climbed out and Deshawn instantly followed me back there.

"This ain't about Erica, you're the one I'm married t—where the fuck did you get all this luggage?" His voice raised an octave as he took in my new Gucci suitcase and duffel bag in horror. "I know damn well you didn't use my card for this shit!" he shouted, and I couldn't stop myself from chuckling.

"Nigga please! You'd noticed if I had spent even a penny out that funky ass account let alone thousands, if you even got that!" Surprised by my outburst, his mouth flopped open and closed a few times and I left his dumb ass standing there. I'd been hoping he was at work so I could come and have a few hours to think over my decision. I didn't want to be rash, and despite the fact that my little fling with Shai only lasted a few days, I considered us even, but him jumping down my throat was igniting my fight or flight response and I wasn't in the mood to fight.

"So, who bought that shit? You think you can just come in here after not coming home or talking to me for three whole days!" He'd gotten his bearings and was now following me inside the house where I instantly turned up my nose. It smelled like the trash hadn't been taken out so I knew his ass hadn't been cleaning. My suspicions were confirmed when I entered the living room and saw multiple restaurant bags around. "Do you hear me! Was you down there fuckin' with one of them Kodak Black lookin' muthafuckas! Huh!"

"Deshawn, you really got some nerve yelling at me when you're the one that's been cheating, and then when I take a few days to process that information I have to walk into a smelly ass house 'cause you can't even clean up behind yourself!"

"I shouldn't have to clean *shit*! My *wife* should've been home! That's your job! I'm the breadwinner, all I should have to do is provide and you do the rest!" My mouth fell open at the stupid shit he'd just said. *Let a nigga get one fat check and he gone switch up on your ass if he ain't a real one.* My mama's words rang in my head. She'd told me years before that Deshawn was the type of nigga that would let me build him up and then show his ass once he was on top, and that's exactly what it seemed like he was doing. Fuck the fact that I had been cooking, cleaning, and bringing home the bacon for the last few years while he barely made enough to cover the mortgage, but now that he had a few zeroes in his bank account he was acting brand new. He'd be sick if he knew I'd been down in Miami fucking on a real rich nigga though.

"Excuse me? I know you ain't say what I think you just said to *me*, the muthafucka that was riding with you before you ever had any money! You're complaining about some luggage that my best friend bought during a shopping spree to cheer me up after the shit you did." Hearing that Sevyn was the who'd bought the luggage had his expression softening a bit.

"Okay, my bad. I probably should've put some more effort into introducing the whole Erica thing on you—"

"Uhhh, you think." I tilted my head, looking at him crazy as hell.

"I honestly wanted to sit down with you and discuss us polygamous—wait, hear me out!" he shouted at my back because I'd walked away. If I didn't remove myself from within arm's reach of him, I'd have been slapping the taste out of his mouth for even suggesting something so ridiculous. Despite it being obvious that I wasn't trying to hear that shit, he still followed behind me, talking himself into a deeper hole. "It's not like it's just for me, think about it. It'll be three incomes, I won't have to bother you for sex all the time, and she could be our surrogate so we wouldn't have to pay some stranger thousands—"

"Do you hear yourself right now? I thought you were the breadwinner? Why in the fuck would we need a third income when you just said you make enough to maintain the house? And I don't need a fucking surrogate! You sound stupid as hell!" The way my husband was talking, I would've thought he was on drugs because he'd gone from going off on me to trying to convince me to become a sister wife. I wanted so bad to just wheel my luggage right back out of there, but the weather in Chicago was already too chilly for any of the things I had packed.

"I'm trying to figure out a way to make this work for all of us." He sighed like he was tired. I was sure that juggling a wife and a mistress was hard work, but he was definitely about to be one short.

"Maybe I don't wanna make this work. I want a divorce." I stopped short with my shoulders drooping. *I* was the one that was tired. After what he'd done, I should've been coming home to roses and a new ring or at least an apology, but all I'd gotten was badgered, talked down to, and offered a consolation prize of possibly having the woman he cheated with permanently inserted into our lives to save our marriage. That's how little this nigga thought of me. If that didn't tell me things were over, nothing else would.

A long silence followed as he processed what I'd just said. I thought for sure he was going to try to put up a fight but, of course, he attacked me, with his sorry ass. "Fuck you then, Zuri! Don't come crawling back when you realize I'm the only nigga that wants yo' fat ass!" he spat, and I heard him snatching up his keys and leaving, making sure to slam the door so hard that the walls shook. After everything else he'd said to me, I wasn't even surprised by his harsh words, but it was even more motivation to take my ass upstairs and pack up as much of my stuff as I could and leaving the house I'd worked so hard to make a home for good.

இ

"I told yo' ass that nigga wasn't no good. Wait 'til I see his peanut head ass!" After leaving, I'd ended up at my mama's house since Sevyn was MIA. As soon as she laid eyes on me she knew it was trouble between me and Deshawn and had been going off ever since. I'd caught her right in the middle of cooking and the scent of the spaghetti and catfish had my stomach growling as she moved about the kitchen slamming everything she touched.

"I know, Mmama." I rolled my eyes, wishing she'd hurry up and make my plate instead of fussing.

"Don't roll them beady eyes at me! If you would've listened in the beginning then you wouldn't be here right now sulking over a nigga that look like ET!"

The wine I'd been drinking came shooting out all over the table as I cracked up laughing. "Ma!"

"Whaaaat! It ain't like I'm lying, Zuri. If I hadn't met his daddy at the wedding I'd be convinced that his mama got pregnant by an extraterrestrial. I just know he came out the pussy lookin' like somebody granddaddy and got nerve to cheat on my baby! Tuh!" She was going clean in and while usually I would've tried to stop her, I was going to sit back and enjoy this roast session. "It ain't all on him though, Z. Being hurt is understandable, but you gotta take a long look in the mirror and accept that there were signs God sent you to stay away from that nigga and you chose to ignore every single one of them bitches... and me... and Sevyn...and—"

"I get it Ma, I do," I emphasized when she shot a look of disbelief my way. "I already know I let that nigga get away with too much all in the name of love."

"It's nothing wrong with love, baby. Love is great and all, but love doesn't pay the bills, a man with a job does. Love also doesn't keep a nigga's dick in his pants, discipline does. A man can say he loves you all he wants but does he have enough self-control and respect for you to be committed even when temptation is staring him in the face? I know you always thought I was being hard on Deshawn, and that's because I knew he didn't have the type of qualities that a man worth marrying should have. Plus yo' daddy liked him and that nigga's judgement is way the fuck off," she said, making us both chuckle. "You live and you learn though, and hopefully the next nigga that enters your life has both discipline and respect. And since you know what that doesn't look like, you'll be able to spot it a little easier next time."

My mama had spoken a whole word as always, and this time it hit different because I wasn't automatically on the defense. If I was being honest, Deshawn had done a lot of things that showed his true colors but I'd made the mistake of trying to love his flaws and red flags away. I knew now though that wasn't the kind of work I was trying to do, and damn sure not on my own. My mama had gone back to cooking and was swaying around her island to Anita Baker, with tongs in one hand and a half-empty wine glass in the other. I always loved seeing my mama carefree and enjoying life after everything she'd been through. My phone vibrated on the table as she tried to hit the high note and failed miserably. Seeing my dad's name had me releasing a heavy sigh and grabbing my wine glass so I could go into another room.

Even at my big age I dreaded calls from Kadeem Miller. He was a bitter baby daddy if I ever saw one and constantly accused my mama of everything from being gay to trying to emasculate him during their fifteen-year relationship. Nothing was ever his fault, not even the multiple times he left the city to pursue a musical career, virtually abandoning me and my mother only to return empty handed. He was my father though, and I was thankful that regardless of his faults he wasn't as bad as some fathers.

Sitting down on the couch, I tucked my legs underneath me and accepted the call. "Hey old man."

"Ahh, you got jokes! Ain't nothin' old over here girl, you better ask somebody!" He laughed boisterously and I rolled my eyes. Even though he was in his fifties he swore he still had it like that.

"Nope, I'm good, I don't wanna ask nobody nothing." I shook my head like he could see me, hoping that he did go into a long drawn-out story about some younger woman that wanted him.

"You just don't wanna hear the truth. It's okay if yo' daddy still got it girl, you should be proud." He was still laughing while I was completely disgusted and ready to move on.

"Did you call me for something Dad? 'Cause—"

"Don't be tryna rush me off the phone, girl," he chastised, growing serious. "I'm calling because I ran into Deshawn today and he told me you're trying to get a divorce." I sucked my teeth because I should've known that's what his ass had called for. The likelihood that he'd "run" into my husband was slim to none, and either he'd run and told my dad or he had taken his ass over there crying because his mouth had signed a check that his ass couldn't cash.

"I am." I kept it short, not really wanting to discuss this shit with him.

"Come on Zuri, I told you when you first got married that loving a man, especially a black man, is hard. Shit, marriage in general is hard, but you can't go running every time something doesn't go your way." My jaw dropped hearing my father immediately taking Deshawn's side without talking to me first.

"Daddy, Deshawn sticking his dick in another woman is not a part of the trials and tribulations of marriage and I don't have to accept it. Next time you see his ass, tell him to let Erica deal with loving his black ass!" I shouted, hanging up before he could say anything else. I knew I'd have to hear his mouth about it later, but for now I was done with any conversation about my soon-to-be ex-husband.

SHAI A'SANTI

K nowing we'd touched back down, Casa had insisted we stop through. I was still pretty relaxed after spending the last three days with Zuri so I was hoping this meeting wasn't going to fuck that up. We'd been attached at the hip since the night we saw each other at the club, and as much as I wanted to pretend that I didn't like having her ass around, I couldn't. That's one of the reasons why I was relieved to see that the friend she'd run off to meet actually existed and wasn't her nigga. Sevyn was cool and the fact that she'd immediately caught Zaakir's interest was a huge plus for me. She kept his ass occupied while I got to spend time alone with Zuri.

Being able to get better acquainted with her only made me like her more, but it was obvious her fuck ass nigga had fucked her up. She was self-conscious about her weight and her looks, even though she was prettier than a bitch and her body was insane. As smart as she was, she'd allowed that nigga to fuck with her mental so bad that she was doubting herself. That's why I spent those three days fucking and spoiling her every chance I got. It felt good doing shit for a person that appreciated it, and it felt even better making her pretty ass smile knowing that she was genuinely grateful.

Regardless of our connection, we never spoke about keeping in touch and I'm sure that was more so because she had plans to return to her nigga, and while I was confident as fuck, I wasn't in a position to put myself out there to get played again. Especially by a woman that was unable to leave a relationship with a fuck nigga. I was cool with the time we'd spent together though and hoped it at least made her force her man to step his game up.

Shaking thoughts of Zuri from my mind, I pulled into Casa's driveway at the same time as Zaakir. It was September so the weather was fluctuating between super-hot and chilly. Since today was the latter, I stepped out of my truck in black Nike joggers and a matching hoodie. I'd barely been able to get showered and dressed after returning from the airport when my uncle called, so I'd thrown on the first thing my hands touched and that included the socks and house shoes on my feet.

"Booooy, what are those!" As soon as Zaakir brought his childish ass around he was pointing and trying to clown the black leather slippers that were lined with brown fur. I'd just left his ass and already he was starting with his bullshit.

"Fuck you nigga!" I grit, shoving my hands down into my pocket as I made my way to the door.

"I don't know what type of switch got flipped in yo' old ass when you turned thirty, but I hope that shit ain't hereditary." He cackled, continuing to make jokes as he followed behind me. "Yo' ass sound like somebody old diabetic granny walkin' around in them bitches!"

I looked at him dryly before turning to ring the bell because his ass stayed talking shit. Before I could even reach for it though, the door was swinging open.

"What's up, Unc?"

"Don't what's up Unc me. Get y'all asses in here." Casa was already wearing a mug as he stood in the doorway in some damn red, silk pajamas.

"Oh hell naw! Both y'all niggas out here lookin' like y'all

bouta go to a smoke lounge!" Zaakir cracked, crossing the threshold.

"Fuck is you talkin' 'bout, this shit nice!" Unc frowned and rubbed a hand down the fabric as if to prove that it was high quality, even though that shit didn't mean nothing to his son. "I bet I could fuck yo' bitch in it, lil' nigga!"

"Ha! Yo' old ass couldn't snatch one of my hoes even if you offered them that sugar daddy money!"

"Oh, that shit dead anyway. I ain't never paid for pussy and I damn sure ain't payin' for none of the lil' pissy ass hoes you meddle with!" They continued going back and forth and I tuned their asses out as we all headed to the living room. Casa and Zaakir's relationship was more like friends than father and son, and they could sit and talk shit for hours if you let them. They were close though and one of the only father-son relationships that I'd been able to witness up close. It was the same type of bond I had with my OG, besides the fact that I wouldn't dare say half the shit to her that Zaakir's ass said to Casa.

I dropped into one of the huge leather chairs Casa had furnished the room with and pulled out my phone to keep me occupied until they finished fucking around. I had a few missed calls, one of which was from my mama, and I made a mental note to drop through and see her after I left, but the others were from two different unsaved numbers. Right away I knew that was Kendra's ass playing on my phone again. Curiosity had me checking the voicemail she'd left and I immediately noticed the change in her usually whiny ass tone. She obviously still hadn't gotten the hint that I wasn't fucking with her, but the next time she called I'd make sure she did.

"Ayite, ayite, I called y'all over here for a reason and yo' lil' goofy ass done distracted me with yo' bullshit," Casa finally said, snatching my attention. I stuffed my phone back in the pocket of my hoodie and waited to see what he was about to say as Zaakir plopped down on the couch across from me.

"I ain't distract shit, yo' ass just old and forgetful... you 'bout getting Alzheimer's and shit. Don't think I'm gone be wiping yo' ass when you forget how to do that shit either," Zaakir told him, never taking his eyes off the phone in his hands as he texted away.

"Ayite, enough jokes now, we got some important shit to discuss. Put that phone away, nigga." Grumbling, Zaakir did what he said, tucking his phone into the side of the couch. Unc waited until it was out of sight before continuing. "Ayite, now you boys have a shipment coming up in a couple days and I wanna make sure we got all the details ironed out, but first, that nigga KG already going around running his mouth about what happened. My source at the police department said even his mama came down there trying to throw yo' name in the mix. Thankfully, he was the one that she approached, so the information she provided ain't going no further than him, but I just need you to know that we might have to take some drastic measures if they keep this shit up." The look he gave told me exactly what he meant, and I sighed. Killing that nigga's pops was one thing, but to kill his mama was something else entirely. It wasn't something I was looking forward to, but I'd do whatever needed to be done to keep my ass out of jail.

"Ayite, Unc." I nodded, swiping a hand over my unruly curls.

"I'ma keep my ear to the streets for now, but nigga," he paused, raising a brow at me, "the next time yo' dangerously in love ass kill somebody over a bitch, *don't*." The warning was clear and while we hadn't gotten out of the situation yet, I knew there wasn't going to be a next time.

"You ain't gotta worry about that. I ain't takin' none of these hoes serious no more," I told him with finality.

"Awww shit! Welcome to the dark side, bro," Zaakir's simple ass said, cheesing. Ignoring him, I listened as Casa moved on to what we needed to know about the upcoming shipment. Our supplier, Mateo, had changed our previous method after finding out that one of his men was fucking with his competition. Of course, he'd killed the nigga but he was trying to play it safe just in case they planned on robbing him. Now instead of a dock we were supposed to be getting them from a cargo train. Since shit was switching up, we needed to be prepared so we could get our merchandise without any hiccups, and Unc thought the best way to do that was to do a trial run. We sat for a while talking over which of our men would come with and what time, before he finally dismissed us with a quick glance at his watch. His old ass had seemed like he was rushing the whole time and as we were leaving out, it was clear why. A bad ass red bone stood on his doorstep holding a bunch of shopping bags filled with everything somebody would need to cook. Although it was obvious she was an older woman, she definitely took care of herself and could easily pass for early thirties at best. The only thing giving her away were the light wrinkles in her face and the gray hair peppering her head. Smirking, Zaakir started flirting with the lady while I walked off. I wanted to go home and catch a few z's before going to check on my mama. Just as I climbed behind the wheel, my phone went off with a call and I instantly recognized it as the number Kendra had left a message from. I hadn't expected her to call back so soon, but it was no time like the present to handle this shit. Sliding the icon across my screen, I sighed and prepared myself for the bullshit.

"Kendra—" I started, skipping the pleasantries, but she immediately cut me off.

"Look, I know you don't want to talk to me right now, but it's a reason I've been calling you like this. Do you think you can come over? I really don't wanna get into this over the phone." Just like in her voicemail, it was clear there was something different about her, but instead of feeding into it, I refused.

"No, I told you I ain't fuckin' with you like that. Fuck around and you try and set me up on some funny shit. If you got something to say, say that shit now because this the last time I'm gone oblige you. Stop fuckin' callin' me unless yo' ass wanna end up like yo' bitch ass nigga," I told her just as calmly as if I was telling her the time.

"You know what, I was tryna be nice, but since you wanna talk crazy and threaten me, then fuck it. I'm pregnant! Congratu-fuckinglations!" she huffed, hanging up in my ear. *Shit!*

ZURI ROSS

I t didn't take long for me to find my own place after moving out of the house me and Deshawn shared and into my mama's. It was a cute little two-bedroom condo a few houses down from Sevyn's and I was in complete love with the size and how I'd decorated it. Deshawn had always refused to let me add color to our home, wanting only black furniture and matching decorations, while I was a statement piece type of girl.

Every room was different and had its own vibe. I'd chosen a cream, peach, and rose gold theme for my living room. In my bedroom, I went with a royal blue circle bed with silver accents and mirrored nightstands and dressers. I even had a cute little design on the wall behind my bed like I'd seen on TikTok. To say I was thriving was an understatement. It seemed like everything was falling into place for me and the only thing holding me back was Deshawn's unwillingness to cooperate with the divorce.

I'd filed the same week that I left him and he still hadn't signed the papers. First, he claimed he needed to get a lawyer to look over them, and then he insisted he get to keep the house instead of selling it and we split the profits. He'd even asked for my ring that we'd gone half on back. The most ridiculous thing he'd done was request spousal support since I'd been the breadwinner for so long. It really didn't make sense for him to be so childish, but I shouldn't have expected anything less from a man that had already done so much to me.

Surprisingly, none of his antics had the wanted effect on me though. He was trying to break me, even going so far as to move Erica into our damn house, but I still wasn't bothered like he wanted me to be. She could have him and all of his alpha male bullshit.

A knock on my door had me sitting up in bed and instantly falling back into my pillows from the dizzy spell that hit me. I'd been feeling like crap for the last few days and had confined myself to my bed in hopes that some Tylenol flu and soup would get me back to normal. So far nothing had helped. I was days in and still couldn't keep anything down or move around without getting dizzy. I'd been convinced it was food poisoning and then I was convinced it was a stomach flu, but Google said that didn't last any longer than one to three days.

When none of my remedies worked, I called my mama and she didn't hesitate to tell me she was making me some of her special vegetable beef soup and coming over. I knew it was her at the door because it had been a few hours since I'd talked to her. A second later, a poorly written text came through my phone from her, confirming my suspicions. Pushing through the dizziness I was feeling, I walked to the door slowly so I wouldn't make my symptoms worse.

"Oh wow, you look a mess!" my mama quipped with her nose turned up as soon as I opened the door.

"Woooow, thanks Ma." I had avoided looking in the mirror because I already knew I looked a mess, but she definitely didn't have to point it out.

"Quit being so sensitive Zeebee, I'm just saying that you look really ill. Maybe you should go to the doctor." She called me by my childhood nickname, probably to lighten the blow of the insult.

Frowning, I accepted the Tupperware bowl she was holding

out to me and shook my head. The last thing I was trying to do was sit in the doctor's office, especially if I may be contagious. Besides, if I went up there and all they told me was that I had to let it run its course, I was going to be pissed. "I don't feel like going out Ma, maybe tomorrow." I was already headed to the kitchen to warm up the soup. Throwing up had my throat raw as fuck and I was hoping the hotter it was the more soothing it would be.

As soon as I opened the top, my stomach growled and I prayed that I'd be able to keep it down. Sitting down at the table, I dug in and moaned at how good it felt and tasted sliding down my throat. A couple bites in, my stomach flipped violently and I knew everything I'd just eaten was about to come up. Slapping a hand over my mouth, I shot out of the kitchen and tried to make it to the bathroom but fell to my knees right at the door. Since I'd only gotten in a few slurps not much came up, but the painful dry heaves afterwards were the worst part. I don't know how long I was on my knees before my mama came in talking shit.

"See yeah, yo' ass need to go to the doctor 'cause I know damn well my soup ain't fuck with yo' stomach like that. Gone, take a shower and I'll drive you," she huffed, disappearing from the doorway and returning a second later with some clean towels. This time I didn't even try to argue, as she helped me up from the floor. At least I could ask the doctor for some medicine to stop me from throwing up, because I honestly didn't think I'd be able to make it any longer without eating.

We ended up going to a fast care that wasn't too far from my house, and I was immediately happy to see that there weren't very many people there. It didn't take long to get signed in and a few minutes later I was escorted to an exam room with my mama in tow. As soon as the door closed behind us, she immediately started rummaging through the cabinets and drawers. "Girl, what are you doing?"

"Uh *girl*, what it look like? I'm shopping. Why buy this stuff when they got plenty?" She shrugged, throwing Band-Aids and alcohol pads in her purse. I couldn't even do shit but laugh as she stole everything from Kleenex to sticky notes before sitting down and crossing her legs. It was right on time too, because not even a second later there was a tap at the door and a middle-aged white woman entered.

"Hello, I'm Doctor Graham. I heard you were having some stomach issues? Wanna tell me exactly what's going on?" she asked, barely looking up from her notepad.

"Uh yeah, I've been having some nausea and dizziness. I thought maybe it was food poisoning but once it hit day three I thought it might be a virus. None of the things I've taken are helping and I still can't keep anything down." Not being able to eat had me ornery. Not only was I a foodie but I was also a thick girl, and I didn't appreciate the way my stomach had been acting up on me.

"Well, I can certainly understand your frustration. Now, we can definitely rule out food poisoning since it's been so many days, but I also don't think it's a virus either." She glanced at my mama before shifting her eyes to me. "Do you mind me asking when is the last time you had sex?"

Confused, I looked at her ass like she was crazy before it dawned on me. She thought I was pregnant! Dizziness hit me as I shook my head roughly. "I'm *not* pregnant. I haven't even had sex in months to *get pregnant*. Plus, I've been having my period regularly."

"You're damn right you're not!" my mama cut in, garnering a wary look from the doctor who paused before continuing.

"Okay, I hear this a lot and it's a common misconception, but sometimes bleeding is normal in early pregnancy and women often assume it's a regular menstrual but—"

"Look ma'am, I've been pregnant a couple of times in the last few years and I never bled. That's how I even knew in the first place besides my breasts being tender. Morning sickness isn't even one of the symptoms I get." I cut her off even as my mind wondered. There was no way I'd spent the last year trying to get pregnant by Deshawn's ass again to save our marriage only to pop up pregnant during our divorce. The last thing I wanted was any ties to that man, but after suffering through miscarriage after miscarriage, I couldn't see myself getting rid of this blessing. My head thumped as she continued on, seemingly getting excited for me while I was trying hard not to cry.

"Every pregnancy is different, Zuri. One baby may give you every symptom and another may not give you any. Were any of your symptoms present throughout the pregnancy?" she probed in an understanding tone.

"No... I uh, I never carried to term." My eyes shifted in shame.

"Ohhhh." I could already hear the pity in her voice and I dreaded looking up to see that same expression on her face. "I'm sorry to hear that. Let's just run the test to be sure and then we'll go from there."

"Zuri, I know damn well you ain't been out here fuckin' yo' raggedy ass husband," my mama chastised as soon as the lady left the room.

"What, no! Didn't you just hear me tell her I haven't had sex in months? If I'm pregnant it's from when we were on vaca— ohhhh shit." The cruise and all of the events that happened during it flooded my mind before Shai's face popped up. We'd spent a majority of the time we were together fucking and while we had been careful, we might have had one or two slip ups. The fact that it was within days of me being with my husband, there was no telling who the father could be if I even was pregnant.

"Oh shit what?" she huffed, looking at me with her forehead bunched irritably, ready to curse me the fuck out depending on what my answer was. Just like I'd left the threesome out of the story, I'd left out the fact that I'd spent a few days afterwards letting a nigga I didn't know fuck the shit out of me. Hell no!

Thinking quickly on my feet, I said, "I was just thinking that it could be from then. We weren't using protection." Her face showed her skepticism, but she didn't call me out. After a few seconds, she released a heavy sigh.

"Well, I can't say that babies aren't blessings and I know you don't want to be a single mother, but I hope if you are pregnant you aren't considering getting back with that nigga. Y'all can coparent but do not let his troll ass convince you to drop this divorce."

"Oh no, me and Deshawn are done. There's no coming back from the things he did," I said firmly, and I meant that. If I was in fact pregnant, I'd keep it just because there was a chance it would survive, but as far as being a family that would never happen. Seemingly satisfied with that, she sat back in her seat while we waited for a nurse to come and help me with the test.

Approximately a half hour later, the doctor's suspicions had been confirmed and we were leaving with a prescription for prenatal vitamins and Dramamine. While my mama went on and on gushing about possibly being a grandma, I sat staring out the window, hoping that I hadn't accidentally conceived a child with a man I was no longer in contact with.

ZURI ROSS

I t had been a week since I found out I was pregnant and my Ob/Gyn hadn't wasted any time getting me an appointment. Due to my previous pregnancy issues she wanted to monitor the baby right away to make sure there everything was progressing like it should, and I agreed. It took me a couple of days to decide whether or not I wanted to tell Deshawn about the baby. He was already stressing me out with the divorce and the last thing I wanted was for him to ruin my pregnancy with his bullshit, but I'd ultimately told him because he'd suffered behind the loss of our babies too and deserved to be there from the beginning.

Of course, he immediately did what my mama said and tried to weasel his way back in, spouting off statistics of single mothers, but I was adamant that there wasn't going to be a reunion between us. He'd left it alone, but I knew he wasn't done at all even though he was still going strong with Erica.

I pulled into the lot of the new office where my doctor was located and found a spot close to the door for expectant mothers with a small smile. Despite the bullshit, I couldn't lie and say I wasn't excited about the possibility of having a baby. I tried not to get my hopes up but it was hard considering how long it'd taken to get here.

A light tap on my window snatched me out of my thoughts, and I looked up to see Deshawn standing there with a huge grin. He'd been just as excited as I was when I'd told him and honestly, I was surprised. I thought for sure his bitterness behind the divorce was going to have him accusing me of being pregnant by someone else, but he instantly claimed the baby, no questions asked.

"Hey, I wanted to catch you before we went inside," he said nervously once I had my door open. Frowning, I tried to prepare myself for whatever was about to come out of his mouth as I reached around for my purse.

"Okay, but please don't start. I'm in a really good mood and I'm not trying to argue today," I warned, stepping out. His eyes roamed my body in the cream joggers and dark tan fitted shirt I wore with a fuzzy brown and cream-checkered trench coat. It was casual day at work and I took the opportunity to dress comfortably knowing I'd be going to the doctor right after. Deshawn was ogling me like I was in something much sexier though.

"You look great." Blinking, he stepped back so he could get a better look, I guess. I was confused as to why he seemed so enthralled when nothing about me had changed since the last time I'd seen him, besides gaining a pound or two, but that would've normally made him feel the exact opposite.

Unsure of how else I should respond, I shrugged and gave a confused, "Thanks." I wasn't dare going to fix my lips to say the same, even though he still looked very much attractive to me. "Well?" I asked when he still hadn't said anything, and he laughed sheepishly, showing off the one dimple he possessed that used to make me weak in the knees.

"My bad, I uh, I just wanted to see if you uh...wanted your ring back." He threw his hands up to stop the protest that was on the tip of my tongue. "I'm just saying because I know you don't like the whole single mother trope and I'm sure you haven't told

Kim about the divorce yet," he hinted, making my frown deepen. He knew exactly what he was doing, but at the same time I couldn't argue. I didn't like how a lot of people assumed as a black woman that I was unwed and pregnant. I'd gotten it a lot every time when I came for a doctor's appointment, even with my wedding ring visible on my hand. The thought had me irritated just remembering some of the things people had asked me, not really intending to sound prejudice or judgmental but still very much giving off both. Sighing, I looked up toward the building and then back to the hopeful expression on his face. Even knowing that he was using manipulative tactics, I still reluctantly agreed.

"Okay." The words had barely left my mouth when he hurriedly pulled it out of his pocket and reached for my hand. Happily, he slid the modest diamond on my finger before clasping my hand in his and giving it a light tap. Instead of releasing me, he held onto me firmly and started for the door. It was like deja vu walking into the doctor's office holding hands with him while we went to check on our baby, and I instantly got anxiety. As if he knew I was nervous, he gave my hand a little squeeze as we passed all of the other pregnant women. Some were alone, but most of them had their husbands or boyfriends with them and despite hating Deshawn's stupid ass, I was glad that I'd allowed him to come.

It didn't take them long to send me to the back and after giving them a urine sample I was put into a room and asked to change into a gown. Deshawn instantly caught an attitude when I closed the curtain on his dumb ass, but he had me fucked up if he thought I was undressing in front of him, not yet divorced husband or not.

A few minutes later there was a tap on the door before my doctor, Kim James, came in with a smile. "Hello again folks, I hear we're expecting again?" she gushed, and I couldn't stop myself from cheesing as I nodded.

"Yes, I'm hoping this is the one." As excited as I was, I was still very much nervous and she instantly noticed.

"Well, your vitals are looking good so we'll see. Go ahead and lie back so I can check you out," she said, going to the sink and washing her hands before slipping on some gloves while I did as she'd asked. I already knew what was coming next, so I was prepared when her cold fingers entered me as she pressed against my abdomen. "Have you been having any issues?"

"Not really, I was having extreme morning sickness and dizzy spells last week, but I've been taking Dramamine for that and it's gotten much better." Since I'd left urgent care I'd been faithfully taking my vitamins and the nausea medicine and it had definitely made a difference. I was finally able to keep food and drinks down and I hadn't stopped eating since, which is how I'd gained the weight in only a week. Kim nodded with a neutral facial expression as she continued to push and prod me.

"Any pain or cramping?"

From my previous pregnancies, I knew that some light cramping was to be expected in the first trimester so I wasn't alarmed at the question or the fact that I'd had once or twice in the past week, which was what I told her.

"Okay, everything seems good. Let's give the heart a listen." She gave me one of those looks like she was worried I'd have a mental breakdown if anything didn't sound right, and she was absolutely correct. I tried to take slow steady breaths, but it didn't stop my heart from pounding dramatically. Once again, Deshawn was two steps ahead of me, stepping right over and scooping up my hand again with a hopeful expression. Squeezing my eyes shut, I said a silent prayer as she placed the Doppler on my belly. I didn't even realize I'd been holding my breath until the unmistakable whooshing sound filled the room, and I gasped as tears slid down the sides of my face.

I was so overcome with emotion that I didn't even push Deshawn away as he happily peppered kisses on my face. "The heartbeat sounds good and strong, Zuri. It's at 170," Kim informed me with a pleased nod before turning the machine off and wiping the gel off my belly. "Everything's looking good, but

I'm gonna have you come back every week for now. In the meantime, continue to eat healthy and keep your stress down. We're hoping for a full-term pregnancy so we need to take all precautions." She spoke with us a little bit longer before leaving so that the ultrasound tech could come in. Usually I would've went to see them first but since I'd had so many issues before she'd switched things around. Now that we'd confirmed the heartbeat though, we were all set to see our little blob onscreen.

It was bittersweet seeing my baby, because although I was happy there was still the fear I'd never get to hold her or him. The worry had me even more anxious as we left and I stopped at the front desk to schedule another appointment.

"Aw shit, I forgot my keys. I'll be right back," Deshawn mumbled and took off back to the exam rooms, leaving me alone in line. I took my time focusing on my ultrasound as the person ahead of me finished up, but the sound of a familiar voice had me quickly glancing up. My breath instantly caught in my throat and I swear I couldn't breathe seeing Shai. The last thing I ever expected was to see *him* of all people. I'd tried to put the few wonderful days we'd spent together behind me, but seeing him just brought them to mind and I thirstily looked him over. He looked just as fine as the day we went our separate ways. Shit, even better if that was possible. Just like the first night he was in a suit that fit him perfectly, and I bit my lip thinking about his broad shoulders and thick arms hoisting me in the air as he fucked me mercilessly.

"Zuri, baby, you left your prescription back there too," Deshawn's stupid ass said, stepping back in line, and I watched as Shai's body tensed before he turned around and did a double take. Unfazed by my husband's presence, he narrowed his eyes between the two of us for way too long, and for the first time I noticed the woman with him. She was beautiful with cocoa-colored skin and a thirty-inch bust down that was perfectly installed. *Obviously he got a type,* I thought.

"Shai...is the morning good for you on the thirtieth?" She

turned slightly, giving me a perfect view of her full belly, and my gaze shifted back to him. Here I was feeling guilty and this whole time he'd had a woman, a very pregnant woman that he'd obviously cheated on with me. Anger filled me even though I had no real right to be mad. I hadn't asked him if he had a woman or anything, he'd been the one asking questions, and although I had omitted being married he did know I was there nursing a broken heart. I felt taken advantage of and if we weren't in mixed company I would've cursed him the fuck out. "Shai?" She finally looked to see what had his attention and possessively put her hand on his arm and the other on her round belly.

With my eyes locked on his, I raised a daring brow, ready to blow up his spot even as Deshawn pulled me deeper into his side. Shai zeroed in on the contact and I could tell his face tightened, but instead of saying anything he turned his ass back around and finished up before leaving the building without another look in my direction.

I tried to shake off the encounter, but I was still bothered even after scheduling my next appointment. My mind instantly wondered to what lie he was telling his woman about me and I couldn't help being bothered.

"Aye, did you know that nigga back there?" Deshawn quizzed as soon as we'd cleared the building. We'd left literally minutes after the couple but I found myself looking around as if Shai could still be out there. "Zuri, do you hear me!" He sped up, snatching me by the arm when I still hadn't answered in a timely manner.

"I don't know what you're talking about! What nigga?" I played dumb, staring at him angrily. My frustration was for a lot of reasons, but I was hoping he thought it was from him asking me something stupid. His eyes turned to slits as he studied me, I guess trying to see whether I was lying or not. "Let me go, fool, I told you I didn't want you ruining today with your bullshit and the first thing you do is grab on me asking about a nigga I don't know!" I snatched away and he took a step back like he was just now realizing what he was doing.

"Sorry, I just didn't like the way that nigga was staring at you." He sighed, scratching the back of his neck. "You wanna grab some food quick so we can talk about things going forward?"

"No, you've already showed your ass out here and I already have plans with Sevyn anyway. Take yo' ass home to Erica." Sucking my teeth, I dug through my bag for my keys, already starting to head to my car again while he stood there looking stupid. I hurried into my car and pulled off before he could object, wishing that I could have a drink because this shit was too much for me. Seeing Shai with a very pregnant woman made me feel as if it was a good thing I hadn't tried to find him and tell him about my baby possibly being his. Obviously, he had some shit with him just like my husband did, and I didn't want to join any more circuses. *Nope, I was more than good on Shai A'santi.*

SHAI A'SANTI

"So, are you going to tell me who that was?" Kendra continued to question me even though I still had yet to answer her ass. She'd been pressing me since we left her doctor's office and no matter how tight lipped I was, she just kept pushing, irritating me even more than I already was. "Shai!" she shouted, gaining a hard stare from me that actually shut her stupid ass up.

"A bitch I was fuckin' in Miami," I told her truthfully, enjoying how her face fell. She knew better than anybody that you shouldn't ask questions you weren't ready for the answer to, so her hurt feelings were on her. "Happy now?" I taunted as her lip quivered.

"No, I'm not happy! Why would you say that! Is she really?" she asked in a small voice that didn't match her usually boss bitch vibe, and I snorted. She'd definitely switched up since getting pregnant and had turned into a soft-hearted crybaby.

"Didn't I just say she was? Stop asking questions you don't really want the answers to, Ken. We're *not* together so hurting yo' feelings ain't a concern of mine," I sneered, regretting that I'd agreed to drive her dumb ass instead of letting her drive herself. Since she'd told me she was pregnant, she'd become extremely needy and was leaning on me hard as hell hoping this baby would bring us back together, although there was a chance it could be Kyrie's. She was taking my kindness as a sign that we were working toward being together for the baby when that was the furthest from the truth. If anything, me not being one hundred percent sure that the baby was mine was only a testament about how little I could trust her thot ass.

"I know we're not, you make sure to tell me that all the time. I know I fucked up but you don't have to throw bitches in my face, Shai!" she cried as tears streamed down her face, instantly blowing the fuck out of me. I wasn't in the mood for her theatrics, especially when I was already pissed off from seeing Zuri. *A married or engaged Zuri!*

For some reason, I just knew the nigga with her was the same one who had her in Miami broken and looking for some type of affection. To know that even after I'd shown her how a nigga was supposed to treat her she'd still gone back to his ass had me heated, and it didn't help that she looked even better than she had months ago. I knew damn well that nigga hadn't given her that glow. Even when he tried to step up, his ass still looked lame as fuck and hadn't even had the balls to say shit about me openly staring his woman down. *Bitch ass!*

This was the exact reason why I wasn't trying to take her goofy ass seriously. Wasn't no way a nigga that had her crying to a perfect stranger was deserving of her hand in marriage, and I hated that she'd fallen for whatever bullshit he'd told her to get her back. A part of me wanted to say fuck her and put her ass out of my head, but she'd been living in my brain rent free since I left her, so that was easier said than done, especially when I felt like God had placed her in my path a second time.

"Shai, are you listening? I'm over here pouring out my heart and you don't even care!" Kendra whined, cutting into my thoughts. "I love you, and I know I made a mistake but I'm trying my best to get us back on track. This baby is a sign and—"

"That baby could be a dead nigga's baby, so stop with the bullshit."

"I wish you'd stop saying that."

"And I wish you'd take the paternity test so we'd know for sure, but you won't," I shot back, making her mouth tighten defiantly. "But you're trying to hang on to this shit for as long as you can just in case it's not mine. I get it, but you're wasting your time, Ken. Whether it's mine or not, we ain't getting back together so you might as well get that shit through yo' fucking head!" I'd been saying the same shit since she announced her pregnancy and it seemed like it was going in one ear and out the other every time. She was thinking that my presence meant something for her when all it meant was on the off chance that the baby was mine, I wanted to be there from start to finish. I wasn't trying to be a fuck nigga like my pops, even if I didn't want to be with the mama, but she wasn't understanding that. She was really setting herself up for a huge let down, but that was on her.

"I know it's your baby, Shai," she said weakly, and I shrugged.

"Then you shouldn't have no problem taking the test, Kendra." My tone was condescending, and it instantly had her flustered.

"I will once it's here, but I don't think I should put my body through that just to find out something we can wait a few more months for." Once again, I shrugged indifferently. She was willing to die on the hill just to spend time with me, and I prayed her delusional ass tendencies didn't trickle down to the baby.

"Ayite," I said with finality, cutting up the radio to dead any further conversation, and her mad ass folded her arms and stared out the window. That was fine with me because that was her best bet anyway.

I was relieved a half hour later when I finally pulled up to her crib and instead of trying to linger, she jumped her ass out without a word. Knowing better than to slam my damn door, she shut it lightly and stomped up the walkway to her door. I only waited long enough for her to make it inside and then peeled the fuck off. I was supposed to be having dinner with my OG but after spending the last hour or so with Kendra's ass, I was ready to cancel. I knew damn well Queen wasn't going for that shit though. It had been a minute since I'd been by her house and she was going to pull up on me if I canceled, so I headed home so I could shower and change. Since I didn't live that far away from Kendra, I was pulling up at home a short time later and climbed out of my truck. Knowing my mama, she had already started cooking hours before so the food would be done by the time I made it. The thought of the good eating I was about to do had my stomach growling and put a little pep in my step.

After taking a quick shower, I threw on some dark blue Levi's, a plain white tee, and a blue crewneck sweatshirt. I stepped into some fresh out the box dunks that had the same colors as I was wearing and was ready to go. My phone was ringing before I could make it out the door though, and I laughed seeing my OG's name.

"I'm on my way woman, don't be clockin' me," I said as soon as her face appeared on the screen, instantly making her eyes narrow.

"Oh, they must have been handing out drugs at the doctor's office 'cause I know you ain't talkin' to me," she gawked, making me chuckle.

"Why I gotta be on drugs Queen, you trippin'."

"Naw, yo' ass trippin'. I'm over here waiting on you to eat and you wanna play on the phone." She rolled her eyes hard and I realized her ass was hangry, which made it even funnier. "Boy!"

"Ayite, ayite. I'm on my way though for real. The appointment just took a little longer this time because the baby wasn't trying to open its legs," I informed her, and her face softened just a little.

"That girl still ain't trying to give you no test?" was all she said, completely bypassing the rest. My mama had made it clear from the beginning that she wasn't getting involved in shit until it was proven through DNA that I was the father. She already hadn't liked Kendra, but finding out she cheated on her baby boy made her hate her ass even more and refusing to give me a test was just the icing on the cake. If she knew like I knew though, she'd tread lightly fucking with Queen A'santi because my mama was just as deadly as me even though she looked like a little diva.

"No, she's insisting on waiting until its born so that's what we gotta do. Her body her choice." I shrugged even though I didn't want to be as understanding as I was sounding.

"Tuh, her body bouta be laid the fuck out if she keeps playing with you. These little girls need to learn that a baby don't keep no man and it definitely doesn't when you done cheated on the man." I really wasn't in the mood to get into all that with her at the moment. I'd already just had this annoying conversation with Kendra's bullheaded ass and I was still in a semi-pissed mood over Zuri.

"You can't be threatening that girl, she might be pregnant with yo' grandchild."

"I mean, it's a chance that it's not my grandchild soooo." She shrugged with a roll of her eyes.

"Man, I ain't fuckin' with you, I'll be there in a second." I couldn't help shaking my head at her crazy ass. The reckless mouths clearly ran in my family because every single one of their asses said whatever they wanted and didn't give a fuck about hurting nobody feelings.

"Alright, hurry up before your greedy ass uncle and cousin come eat it all, 'cause you know they not gone wait for your late ass." She hung up before I could even tell her that she better not let them eat shit, but I already knew she wouldn't. Her ass had only said that to rush me.

Climbing behind the wheel of my Mercedes this time, I made the short drive to my mama's crib and saw that both Zaakir and Casa were already there. I quickly parked behind Casa's Bentley and walked up to the door letting myself in. I could hear all of them talking loudly in the back and I went to wash my hands before following the smell of fried chicken, greens, macaroni, and cornbread to the dining room.

"'Bout time nigga, yo' mama wasn't tryna let nobody eat 'til yo' light-bright ass came. I swear y'all be on that colorist shit over here, I'ma disown all y'all," Zaakir fussed from his seat at the table, and my mama instantly slapped his ass on the back of the head.

"Watch yo' god damn mouth, nigga! Just 'cause y'all grown don't mean shit changed, and ain't nobody over here colorist. Stop using words you don't know the definition of."

"Damn Pops, you just gone let yo' sister put her hands on me *and* cuss me out?" Zaakir threw his hands up looking at Casa for help, but that nigga was busy helping himself to a hefty helping of macaroni.

"Sorry son, I already been slumming it just for homecooked meals so I gotta side with sis on this one. Watch yo' damn mouth." The look on his face was dead serious as he said it, making Zaakir suck his teeth while I laughed. That's what his ass got. He was always trying to come for me because I was light skin and he was the one always whining about shit.

"That's what yo' childish ass get." I chuckled, discreetly raising my middle fingers up at him as I took the seat right across from him. My mama popped my ass on the head too though.

"Stop playing with me Shai." She gave me a stern look and I threw my hands up in surrender before digging in. We made small talk as we ate, catching up on regular shit that didn't have nothing to do with business, when her doorbell rang. My eyebrows instantly shot up because as far as I knew, Queen didn't let anybody but us come to her crib. Shooting a look at my mama, I expected for her to be just as confused as the rest of us, but she fought back a smirk and slid back from the table. "I have a surprise for you baby, just wait right here," she said, standing up.

"Aye Aunty, if it's a big booty stripper, I want one too!" Zaakir's stupid ass said, making her roll her eyes.

"Shut yo' ass up," she fussed, disappearing out of the room. I

shared a confused look with Casa, surprised that even he seemed
not to be privy to what she had up her sleeve. Usually my OG
talked with her brother about everything, but obviously she'd
kept this one a secret even from him. I was still facing my uncle so
I saw the way his face tightened at the sight of my surprise and
instantly dreaded turning around, but when Zaakir seemed too
stunned to crack any jokes, I looked over my shoulder.

"Now baby, hear me out," my mama urged when I jumped
out of my seat.

"What the fuck this nigga doin' here, Queen?" If looks could
kill, my bitch ass father would've been one dead ass Italian. The
smile on his face faltered seeing my reaction, and he shifted his
eyes to my mama uncomfortably.

"I thought he knew I was coming."

"Oh nigga please, you know damn well if he knew you were
coming he wouldn't have showed up!" She slapped her thigh frus-
tratedly before turning back to me.

"This is your surprise, Shai. Your father has been trying to get
in touch with you—"

"You for real Ma, you really letting his ass come in here with
this bullshit like he ain't been MIA my whole damn life! I'm
thirty fuckin' years old!" I'd never had a reason to question my
mama, but for her to even be talking to his ass was crazy as fuck to
me. The time that it mattered whether I had a father was long
gone and at my age, there wasn't shit he could do for me but stay
the fuck away.

"If you would just listen—" she started, but I cut her off
quickly.

"Naw, I'm good. I love you Ma, but don't call me over here if
this nigga gone be around." Pressing a kiss to her cheek, I stormed
past them, making sure to shoulder check his goofy ass. I had to
laugh at the fact that there were no men with him like his family
was known to have whenever they were out and about. That let
me know he was still on some secretive shit. How my mama
didn't see it was crazy as hell. A million questions burned through

my mind about how his slick-haired ass was able to get through to her, and why he was even coming around again, but I wasn't thirsty enough for those answers to consider asking her ass. As much as it pained me, I was going to have to keep my distance as long as she was fucking with him. I just hoped she saw what I did sooner rather than later and got the fuck from around him.

ZAAKIR A'SANTI

I'd stopped through my aunt's for some food and had a whole live ass telenovela pop off in the dining room. As soon as Shai's ass left, Queen rushed Giorgio's ass out, but it was already too late. We were all looking at her ass sideways. My pops went into the other room to talk to her while I packed me up two plates to go and a couple for pops too. She'd fucked up the whole vibe bringing that snake ass nigga in there, and I couldn't finish my food comfortably in that atmosphere.

I climbed in my car and carefully set my plates down so they wouldn't leak on my leather seats before going to my contacts list and pressing Sevyn's name. We'd been fucking around since Miami and I couldn't get enough of her cheating ass. She had me out here being a whole homewrecker and shit, which was why I'd kept it to myself that I was even still in contact with her. But the more time I spent with her the more I was ready to officially make her mine. She was still playing that nonchalant shit but regardless of what her mouth said, she answered whenever I called and she always let me come through on the late night.

"What yo' ass want, Zaakir? I just saw you a few hours ago." She tried to play me, but I could hear the smile in her voice.

"Man, cut it the fuck out. You know you was waitin' on a

nigga to call yo' ass!" I found myself grinning too. "You still at the shop?"

"Yesss, you know we stay open 'til 9 on Fridays." At this point I knew her so well, I already knew she was rolling her eyes as she dragged out her words like she was bothered.

"Ayite, I'm on my way. I got a plate for your funny acting ass 'cause I know you ain't ate yet." That had whatever smart shit she was about to say turning into a squeal of happiness. Food was shorty's love language and it often got me in there when she was trying that hard-to-get shit.

"Ooooh okay, see you in a few!" I could hear her gay ass friend in the background asking if it was me, and I smirked. I was becoming a regular fixture in her life and it was only a matter of time before her jail bird ass husband was completely out of the picture.

"Man, ayite." Hanging up, I drove off headed toward her shop. On the way I tried to call my cousin a few times but his mad ass didn't answer and I knew he probably wouldn't until he calmed down. I made a mental note to get up with him later as I pulled up to Sevyn's.

As usual, when I arrived the lot was packed and I shook my head. Shorty was definitely getting to the bag and I had to admit that it was a good look. Grabbing both plates and drinks, I made my way inside, setting off the little bell over the door. As soon as I stepped inside all eyes were on me, and I flashed my teeth at the thirsty ass women that were scattered throughout before spotting Sevyn near her station running her mouth.

"Awww, thank you!" she gushed, rushing over. She looked good as fuck in the black blazer, white crop top, black jeans with tears in the knees, and black sneakers she wore. "Let's go eat in my office."

"Nah uh, Zaaaaakiiiiir! You gone get enough of only bringing food for y'all!" her business partner Tyrese snapped, rolling his neck as he dragged my name like always.

"My bad, I got you next time," I promised, already distracted by the sway of Sevyn's hips as she led the way to her office.

"Mmmhmm," I heard him hum behind me, but he was already in the back of my mind. The door wasn't even closed good and I was setting our food down and pulling her soft body into mine. She smelled just as good as she looked, and I buried my face in her neck with a growl as my hands cupped her ass.

"Stooop, Zaakir! I don't have a lot of time before my next client gets here," she whined but did little to push me away.

"Give me a kiss." I felt like I was begging, but I was thirsty as hell for any type of affection she showed me. She pressed her glossy lips together and quickly tried to give me a peck, but I covered her whole mouth with my own, sticking my tongue inside. My dick was already waking up as she moaned, grabbing the back of my head as our kiss got heated. I was ready to bend her sexy ass over her desk, but I tore myself away. If she only had a few minutes to eat then I was going to let her, because she'd fuck around and work herself to death without taking a second to eat or rest. I shook my head as I pulled back, unable to deny how soft she had me acting, but not being able to stop myself. The shit was crazy for real.

"Asshole," she grumbled, all of a sudden full of attitude, and I laughed, handing her the smaller of the two plates.

"Here man."

She went around to the other side of her desk and grabbed us a couple of plastic forks before taking a seat in her swivel chair. "Mmmm, where you get this from? It's good," she wanted to know as she stuffed her face, barely coming up for air.

"My aunty cooked, we were all over there for dinner, but she invited her bitch ass baby daddy so me and Shai left." I didn't feel any way about the information I gave her, but she gasped dramatically with wide eyes.

"Don't be tellin' yo' family business."

"Ain't no business to tell." I shrugged, digging into my own food, unbothered. "You tryna let me slide through tonight though? I'm tryna touch that lil' dangly thing in the back of yo' throat." I was already on to the next topic as I chewed.

"Nigga what!" she cackled. "How you go from talking about yo' family to asking me for head?"

"Easy, now is you suckin' or what?"

"I'll think about it," she hummed, knowing damn well I was getting the head I requested, judging from the smirk she wore. Before I could call her out, her phone rang. The way her face fell let me know it was her bitch ass husband calling. She still hadn't figured out yet that I was the one that had blocked him months ago and I wasn't going to tell her ass either, but I would've done that shit again if he didn't call so fucking often. Rolling her eyes, she mouthed that she was sorry as she accepted the call.

I tried not to listen as she gave him dry ass, one-word responses, but I couldn't help the satisfied smirk knowing that she was getting tired of that nigga. It was only a matter of time before she was going to be completely off his ass.

"No, I'm eating right now. Well tell him to come tomorrow on the regular day!" I felt like a whole bitch sitting there listening to her talk to him and not saying nothing. I'd never done a female like that, but I had seen other niggas do it and that's just how I was sitting there like an obedient mistress. "Fine, tell him to give me thirty minutes!" She sucked her teeth and hung up, looking irritated.

"You straight?" I didn't like how stressed that nigga seemed to make her whenever they spoke. It was like he got off on ruining her day, but I wasn't trying to overstep and nip the shit in the bud because my ego wanted Sevyn to choose to me on her own.

Sighing, she tossed her head back in frustration. "Yeah, Tramel's brother is stopping through to pick up some money for him, so we'll have to do this some other time." I frowned at the fact that she was sending that grown ass nigga money, and that he was rushing her to do so, but didn't comment. I felt dismissed as she began cleaning up her food even though I understood. She didn't want that nigga's brother to catch me there eating with her.

Still, I took my time, still forking food into my mouth even when she stood up over me.

"Ughhh, come on Zaakir, I don't have time for this. You have to go now, he'll be here any minute." The urgency in her voice pissed me off. In my mind she was my bitch, so for her to be so pressed behind the next nigga was a blow to my ego, even if she was married to his ass.

"I'm still eating, tell his ass to meet you out there," I said evenly despite fuming inside.

"Don't do this, you know I'm not trying to cause any issues in my marriage!"

"Me sitting here finishing my food ain't gone break up yo' fuck ass marriage. All I'm tryna do is finish my food and I'll leave." Shrugging, I continued forking food into my mouth, unbothered by her standing over me huffing and puffing like the big bad wolf as she continuously checked the time on her watch. I guess she got tired of waiting on me to finish because her goofy ass snatched my plate out from under me and tossed it in the trash can in the corner.

"Now you're done, you can go."

I jumped out of my seat so abruptly that the chair slid back, scraping against the hardwood floor loudly. The movement had her tough ass shrinking, and the evil look on her face became one of concern as I silently stared her down. "You got that, Sev," I finally said, and regret washed over her, but she was too stubborn to back down. Stalking out of her office with her right behind me, I immediately noticed a nigga standing in the middle of the room. All eyes landed on me and Sevyn and a hush fell over the shop. Just from the way his ass was glaring at me, I knew he had to be her husband's brother but I wasn't thinking about his ass. His gaze shifted between me and Sevyn like he was putting two and two together.

"Hey Rome!" she spoke nervously, rushing around me and giving him a quick hug that made me smirk. *Scary ass.*

"Hey *sis*, what you got goin' on?" He kept his eyes on me as I finally walked past them but knew better than to speak to me directly. I clocked his bitch ass right away and as bad as I wanted to tell him what was going on so he could tell his brother, I knew it wasn't my spot to blow up. Pissed about having my meal ruined twice in one night, I left out and headed to Harold's. I'd talked a bunch of shit, but I was beginning to feel like I wasn't cut out for the side nigga life. Sevyn had me ready to kill niggas that hadn't even done shit to me, all to have her to myself when she wasn't even fucking with me like that. Obviously, I was going to have to chill on her for a while, maybe fall into some different pussy, but something definitely had to give.

SEVYN ELLIS

I watched Zaakir's retreating back and sighed, knowing that it was going to take some serious ass kissing to get back on his good side. If I even wanted to get back on his good side. It had only been a few months and he was already starting to switch up. He was completely out of line for the shit he'd just pulled. My heart was still pounding just thinking about how crazy things could've gotten if Rome had said anything to his nutty ass.

"Do bro know you be having niggas in yo' office?" Rome asked in an accusatory tone.

"He's a potential client." The lie came out so smoothly I surprised my damn self. I could see it in his face that he was still skeptical, but I played it cool. "Come on, I don't have a lot of time before my next appointment shows up and y'all already cutting into my lunch. I hope you know you're reimbursing me too," I quipped with an attitude. Thankfully, his face broke into a slight grin as he started toward my office.

"My bad sis, it's an emergency, but you know I got you."

"Mmmhmm." I rolled my eyes playfully, breathing a sigh of relief, and followed him back as Tyrese's dramatic ass fanned himself. He wasn't any fucking help, but at the same time this wasn't his issue to help with. It only took a few minutes for me to send Rome on his way with the duffle bag of money that he'd come for after a little bit of small talk. I was grateful he didn't bring up Zaakir again and just left. Hopefully, that meant he'd put the shit out of his mind. Drained from the whole ordeal, I dropped into my chair and sighed just as there was a light tap on the door.

"Girl, that was a close one! Why would you have Zaakir here if you knew they were doing pickups today?" Tyrese entered and sat down in the seat Zaakir had just been in, clutching his flat chest.

"Obviously, I didn't know or else I wouldn't have," I snapped, irritated even though it wasn't his fault. It was Tramel's fault for switching shit up, but I swear it was like that nigga had an inner alarm clock that had him calling me at the most impromptu times. He'd always called often, but whenever I was with Zaakir it was as if he knew that shit and turned it up a notch. Him getting randomly blocked a couple months ago had made his tracking of me worse, and for the life of me I still couldn't figure out how it had happened, but he was convinced I'd done it to be sneaky, which was crazy because if I wanted to not talk to him, I could've just ignored his aggravating ass.

"Uhhh, don't be getting smart with me because you almost got caught up, hoe!" Tyrese sucked his teeth. "I done told yo' ass if you're done with that nigga be done with him and just be with Zaaaaakkiiiirr's fine ass," he said like it was the easiest thing in the world despite knowing my situation.

It wasn't as simple as filing for a divorce and moving out like Zuri had done. Tramel had been drilling it in my head since day one that the reason he was in prison was for me, and to an extent that was true. He'd started hustling back when we were younger after I'd told him about my dream of opening up a shop, and he didn't hesitate to make that happen for me. Being young and in love that just made me more loyal to him, and when he ended up getting put in prison for his crimes it never affected me. I'd kept my shop, my freedom, and our home, and as a token of appreciation, I'd allowed him to start using my shop as a front. The feds thought they'd put a stop to Tramel's drug ring, but he'd just switched it up and now his right hand Rome was running it and washing money through my shop. So, there was no easy out for me, if I wanted to leave him. He'd made sure to bind me to him by the one thing I loved most.

"You know I can't do that. Besides, why leave the devil I know for a new one, especially when Zaaaaakkkiiiir, doesn't even know what he wants." I mocked him and he rolled his eyes.

"It's obvious what that man wants, hoe. He's constantly letting you make the rules and playing this side nigga role when you know that's not easy for a man like him. I just knew for sure he was about to tell the world y'all business just now and beat Rome's ass. You ain't peep it, but he was looking at that nigga *daring* him to question some shit. Ooooh! It had my juices flowing!" Tyrese shivered and fanned himself, making me bust out laughing. That much was true though. Zaakir wasn't like my last nigga, and I knew it was only a matter of time before he got fed up with what was going on and decided to air me out or walk away altogether.

"First of all, nigga, you ain't got no juices and second of all, the minute I feel like things are getting too deep, I'll let him go and move on to the next," I lied, moving around papers on my desk to avoid the knowing look on Tyrese's face.

"It's already too deep boo, and yo' bubble gone burst like that submarine that went down to look at the Titanic if you don't get a handle on this shit." Before I could reply my phone was going off again, and I rolled my eyes seeing that once again Tramel was calling. I answered quickly like I'd been conditioned to do while waving Tyrese's ass out.

"Yes, Tramel." I didn't try to hide my annoyance. He'd already ruined my lunch and my time with Zaakir, so I couldn't understand what he was calling for now.

"How'd everything go?" he asked, completely unfazed by my attitude.

"It went fine, just like always. You don't have to keep checking

on me," I let slip out, unable to stop myself to think of the reper-
cussions of pissing him off. There was a long pause as he let my
words sink in, and I held my breath fearfully just waiting for him
to explode.

"I don't know who you think you talkin' to Sevyn, but I
decide when the fuck I wanna check on you and *my* business.
Matter fact, schedule a visit. It's been a while and I'm trying to see
yo' face." He didn't give me a chance to object as he hung up in
my face. Without me agreeing, he already knew I was going to do
it and begrudgingly, I went to set up the visit like he'd said.

۞

I waited until we were done and locking down the shop to finally
try and call Zaakir. I knew he was pissed and I'd tried to put off
my apology for as long as I could, but I wasn't trying to stay in my
big ass empty house alone. Of course, he didn't answer, but he
had me fucked up if he thought he could just ignore me. After
showering and throwing on some tights and a t-shirt, I thought of
the only option I had. Cursing under my breath, I made the damn
near hour-long drive to his house out in Evanston and gave myself
a pep talk when I pulled in his driveway behind his mustang.
Zaakir was just as strong willed as me, so if he didn't want to let
me in there wasn't anything I'd be able to say, but I was hoping he
wanted me just as bad as I wanted him. I brought my phone with
me to the door and dialed his number as I knocked.

"What you want, Sevyn?" I was surprised that he answered
and had to gather myself and remember what exactly I was
supposed to say.

"Come let me in," I said when my mind drew a blank.

"Naw, take yo' married ass home, bro." My nose turned up at
his attempt to be funny. Throwing my marriage in my face wasn't
going to do anything for me though. We both knew I was
married. The line grew quiet and I could hear him puffing on a
blunt as usual, but the sound of a woman's voice had my ears

perking up. I didn't even realize I could be jealous over him until right then, because knowing he'd left me to lay up with another bitch had me ready to tear some shit up.

"Who the fuck is that, Zaakir? You got a bitch over here, is that why you won't let me in?" I shrieked loudly, banging on the door. "Let me in!"

I was so loud a neighbor's dog started barking, and I saw their lights coming on but kept pounding and talking shit at the same time. The door flew open and Zaakir stood on the other side shirtless with just a pair of sweatpants hanging low on his waist and a blunt dangling between his lips.

"Get yo' goofy ass in here!" he grumbled, snatching me across the threshold before slamming the door shut and cutting off the light. "You gone have these white ass muhfuckas calling the police over here. What the fuck wrong with you?"

I felt stupid for showing my ass, but at the same time it had gotten the desired effect. "No, what the fuck wrong with yo' ass! I asked you to let me in and you wanted to play 'cause you got a bitch up in here! Where her scary ass at!" I continued to shout as I walked further inside and up the stairs. If Zaakir had a woman in his house it was more than likely that he was fucking her, so I went to his bedroom first. The lights were out but the TV was on some Tubi movie, lighting up the empty bed. With narrowed eyes, I went searching around his room as he entered casually, carrying a strawberry crunch ice cream. Sitting down on the edge of the bed, he watched me tear through his room with a smirk.

"You done? 'Cause I'm tryna watch this movie," he asked nonchalantly once I came up empty. I hated how fine his ass was. The nigga even chewed sexy and I wished it was my pussy he was smacking on.

"You can't blame me, I thought I heard a woman up here." Folding my arms, I glanced at the screen.

"You trippin' bro, obviously ain't no bitch up here and if it was, you couldn't say shit about it anyway. In case you forgot, yo' ass married!" he snorted, finishing up his ice cream and sliding back on the bed getting comfortable.

"I'm sorry okay, I shouldn't have thrown your food away, I just didn't want issues in my shop," I tried to explain as he pressed play on the remote, starting his movie back up without acknowledging anything I'd said. The girl on the screen began talking and I realized that was the voice I heard, making my ass feel even dumber. "Are you going to say something?"

"I don't know what the fuck you want me to say. Yo' ass did the most earlier and you want me to just say, *oh well, shorty was having a bad day*? Fuck outta here!" His face balled up as he spoke, letting me know just how mad he was. Kicking off my shoes, I walked over and climbed into the bed, straddling his lap.

"I'm sorry," I mumbled, placing kisses all over his face while he just sat there stoically even as his dick flexed beneath me. "Say you forgive me, baby." Grinding against him, I sucked his bottom lip in my mouth, already feeling myself getting wet in anticipation of him fucking me. Zaakir didn't say a word, but he did engage in the kiss, gripping my ass roughly as his dick grew even harder. I broke away long enough to take off the oversized shirt I was wearing, and he wasted no time latching on to my breasts. Biting my lip, I couldn't stop the orgasm threatening to erupt from the pressure on my clit as I rotated my hips faster.

"You're such a freaky ass lil' bitch," he said almost so low I didn't hear him over the people talking on the screen. Teasingly, he pinched one nipple while sucking the other tenderly, and I couldn't hold it any longer.

"Oooh!" The trembling of my body and the soaked material between us let him know what happened, and he bit my nipple.

"Who told yo' ass to cum?" he demanded, looking up at me with knitted brows. Swiftly, he flipped us over so that he was on top of me. He wasted no time yanking off my tights, as he loomed over me scowling.

"Nobody!" I cried, jerking from the pinch he delivered to my clit.

"Exactly, I tell this fat ass pussy when to cum!" Spreading my legs, he stuck his long fingers inside me and stuck them right in his mouth. "You ain't got no business tasting this fuckin' good," he groaned sexily. Crouching down, he slithered his tongue between my wet folds and I raised my hips to meet him.

"Fuck, Zaakir!" I screeched, reaching for his head, but he slapped my hands away, nastily tongue kissing my pussy, and just before I reached my peak he pulled back and slammed his dick into me.

"Naw, I wanna feel you cumming on this dick Sevyn, and you bet not nut 'til I say so!" he ordered, rocking in and out of me at a tantalizing pace. Wildly I tried to keep up, scratching at his back.

"Ooooh, right there! I'm—mmm!" I whimpered, squeezing my muscles tighter around him.

"This what you wanted, Sev? Huh, dick on demand right!" He leaned down to drop a sloppy kiss on me before burying his face in my neck and switching his movements to a slow grind that had me ready to climb the walls. It felt like his dick was hitting every inch of my pussy and it was...amazing. Wrapping my arms around his neck, I sniveled.

"Please!"

"Fuuuck!" His voice came out muffled as he cupped my ass from underneath me, allowing him deeper.

"Baaaby," I whimpered as my stomach tightened. I could feel my orgasm from the tips of my toes and knew I was right on the edge. "Please!"

Sitting up slightly so that he could look in my face, he smirked. "Let me feel that pussy rain, baby." On demand, my body released and I came hard as my juices gushed between us. "Fuuuck, where you want this nut at?" he grunted, face twisted as he continued his steady pace but now with shorter and more jerky movements.

"In my mouth, I wanna taste it," I said huskily, and he cursed under his breath before pulling out. He moved until he was straddling my chest and I hungrily opened my mouth, angling so that I had more leverage. With the skill of a professional head doctor, I slurped and slobbed until he was shooting his seeds off down my throat, making sure not to waste any.

Dropping down next to me, he closed his eyes panting, and I snuggled up next to him laying on his chest and enjoying the way his heart pounded in my ears. This was what I was afraid of. I was getting way too comfortable popping up at his house and trying to cuddle after sex. Those were big no no's when you were a married woman, but it was almost like I couldn't help myself. Everything with Zaakir came so naturally. I couldn't keep this up and keep my feelings in check. Something had to give. I felt myself beginning to drift off, but he shook me awake with determined eyes.

"Naw, wake yo' ass up. I ain't done punishin' that pussy yet!" What was crazy was how as soon as he said that, I was no longer tired. My thirsty ass climbed right on top of him ready and willing. I needed to get my shit together and fast, because Zaakir was quickly working his way into my head and heart.

ZAAKIR A'SANTI

I woke up to an empty bed and immediately got an attitude, and then I got pissed for having one in the first place. Sevyn's ass had me out here like a straight up mistress for real, all up in my feelings because her musty ass didn't stay the night. I checked the time on my nightstand and saw that it was going on nine in the morning, irritating me more. I'd learned Sevyn's schedule a minute ago so I knew her shop wasn't opening until the afternoon since it was Saturday. There was no reason for her to have gotten up so early. Sitting up, I noticed quickly noticed her clothes were still in the middle of the floor, and like the true sap ass nigga I was turning into, I grinned happily. I knew without a doubt that if Casa's ass saw me he'd never let me live it down.

Shaking my head, I headed to the bathroom to see if she was in there and to relieve myself. The fact that the door was closed let me know she was and as I got closer, I could hear her talking in a hushed tone. I prepared myself to act a damn fool if she was in my shit talking to her bitch ass husband.

"Awww, I'm sorry friend, but I'm voting team Shai on this one. At least if he's the father you know he'll do right by you and his baby even if y'all ain't together. Don't not tell him, that could be his baby too and the last thing you want to do is deprive him of a chance to be there." I couldn't even process the fact that I was happy her ass wasn't talking to that nigga because the news that Zuri might be pregnant by my cousin had my head swimming. The nigga talked all that shit and then went and possibly had two women pregnant at the same time. I made it up in my mind that I was telling his ass as soon as possible, since it seemed like Zuri was on some funny shit, as I opened the door.

Sevyn was at the sink looking in the mirror and damn near jumped out of her skin seeing me there. Smirking, I walked over to the toilet, dick slinging, and started to pee as she sputtered, trying to rush Zuri off the phone.

"Don't stare at my dick, Sevyn." I could feel her eyes on me even though I had my shit closed.

"Well don't come in the bathroom asshole naked and start pissing in front of me," her smart mouth ass shot back. Finished, I flushed and put the seat back down, electing to start the shower instead of washing my hands while she stood there staring at me hard.

"We need to get some things straight, Zaakir," she finally said while I stood next to the shower stall, waiting on the water to get to my liking. Her little attitude was funny as hell to me when she was the one who was in the wrong. She was married to that nigga, so she was the only one worried about his jail bird ass feelings.

"Oh yeah, what's that?" I tilted my head, amused.

"We need to be more careful. I like what we have, but it's obvious that we're both getting too comfortable and that can't happen. I'm not leaving my husband and I also don't want him to find out about this." She tried to make her voice stern but it didn't come off well considering that she was standing in my bathroom stark naked with my cum dried on her thighs.

"You tryna convince me or you, Sev?" I asked, resisting the urge to laugh at the goofy look on her face. "I'm good, you're the one that came over here begging a nigga to forgive you. I was cool with leaving shit where it was." It was a big ass lie. I might've tried to stay away from her ass and fuck other bitches, but the shit was harder than it sounded. My ass had tried to call one of my old shorties the night before and I immediately couldn't go through with it because she was getting on my nerves after a few minutes of talking on the phone. I'd gotten used to Sevyn's nonchalant attitude and dry sense of humor and now everybody else seemed to pale in comparison, which was why I hadn't been in touch with any of my hoes in months. I wasn't stupid enough to tell her ass that though.

"Oh nigga please, you're just as invested in this as I am." Her cocky ass scoffed. "You could've let your neighbors call the police last night and stayed out of it but you didn't, and I ain't hear one complaint when I was up here *begging* as.you put it. So stop tryna play me." She rolled her eyes and planted her hands on her thick hips like she was daring me to lie. Even though I could've let her know that the HOA on my block didn't play that police shit, I let her make it, shaking my head with a grin.

"Okay, so what you sayin' then?" I opted to get back on track, raising a brow.

"No more lunches, no more calling or talking unless it's about sex, and no more fucking me into a coma so I stay here instead of going home." The list she ticked off was immediately unacceptable, especially since besides the lunch thing, she was the one initiating all that shit. Well, maybe I did make it a mission to fuck her so good she couldn't get up to leave, but that's just how I delivered the dick. She stood poised to argue, but I clearly surprised her when I nodded with a shrug.

"Cool."

"Cool?" she gasped with her face balled up. "So that's all you have to say?"

"Yep, you said you wanted dick on demand and that's what you gone get, but you can't be popping up over here either, especially if I don't answer your calls, and you damn sure can't be tryna fight no bitch you catch me with." I laid out a few stipulations of my own that had her frown deepening. Since my water had finally reached the desired temperature, I grabbed a couple of towels and pulled the door open. "Are showers together allowed?" I teased since she still hadn't answered.

"Fine, and yes, showers together are allowed." I knew I'd fucked up her head, but it was obvious that Sevyn's ass was crazy as hell and the only way to combat craziness was with even more craziness. She stomped past me angrily, but despite her attitude she was bent over grabbing her ankles as I gave her deep back shots a few minutes later.

After giving her multiple orgasms, we washed up in silence and went back to my room to get dressed. Instead of slipping back on her dirty clothes, she went straight to my dresser, pulling out a pair of joggers and a t-shirt. I did the same since I was going to stay my ass in the house.

"Make sure you take them cum-stained ass leggings the fuck with you. Don't be tryna leave shit over here or the next bitch gone be wearing them." I laughed at the look of disgust that covered her face. "I should make you wear them bitches home instead of taking my shit."

"You're a dick, Zaakir." She sucked her teeth but made sure to pick up her clothes, folding the leggings up in her shirt to hide the evidence.

"I'm a dick, just call me DOD." I couldn't stop myself from smirking as she scrunched her forehead. "Dick on demand baby, catch up."

"Ugh, you make me sick!" She went to storm off and I didn't stop her. She was going to learn that if she wanted to play games, I'd become the whole damn amusement park. Besides, I needed her ass to leave so I could put my cousin up on game in privacy before I forgot. I watched from my bedroom window as her mad ass got in her car and pulled off like she was hurting anything but her tires as the phone rang in my ear.

"Why the fuck you calling me so early?" he snapped groggily as soon as the call connected.

"I'm calling 'cause yo' ass need to wake up! How you out here with one baby mama and a possible and don't know it? Who waits until their thirties to get reckless?"

"What?" He still sounded half asleep so I decided to stop playing.

"Nigga, Zuri's pregnant and from the way that it sounds, she don't know if you or her nigga is the pappy."

"Wait, what?" The sudden alertness in his voice had me wishing I'd called him on FaceTime just to see the look that accompanied that shit.

"Yeaaaah, you heard me right nigga, you might've got Zuri pregnant. Why was yo' ass out there carelessly fuckin' without a condom? You think Queen mad about Kendra, wait 'til she find out about this shit!"

"Shut the fuck up, Zaakir!" he growled, hanging up on me. Laughing, I counted down in my head, knowing he was going to call back once he shook off the fog of sleep, and just like clockwork, my phone was going off in my hand.

"Hello—"

"Nigga, don't play with me. How you get that information?" he cut straight to the chase. I hadn't told him that I was still fucking with Sevyn so I'm sure it was odd for me to call his ass out the blue with some news on a woman he hadn't seen or spoken to in months. I shrugged like he could see me and stepped away from the window so I could go brush my teeth, and realizing that Sevyn had ran her ass up out of there without doing so had me chuckling. She didn't need any hygiene products at my house anyway.

"I might still be fuckin' Sevyn and heard her talking to Zuri about it this morning," I told him, pulling the phone away from my mouth as I brushed.

"That fuckin' bitch! No wonder her ass was lookin' at me all crazy yesterday while she was with that nigga!" I could hear him shuffling around and raised a confused brow. Him running into her and a nigga the day before was news to me, and I was slightly offended he hadn't mentioned it.

"You saw her yesterday?" I asked for clarification with a mouth full of toothpaste and water.

"Yeah muthafucka, when I was at the doctor with Kendra's goofy ass." I'd forgotten all about their appointment to find out the sex of baby question mark, but the fact that he'd run into Zuri at the same doctor was funny as hell.

"Daaaaamn, that's crazy for real."

"You think Sevyn will give you her address or phone number or something?" he quizzed, still making all types of noise as he moved around.

"Hell naw, nigga I was eavesdropping! I ain't tellin' on myself to help yo' ass out!" Once again, his sassy ass hung up on me and I made a mental note to slap the fuck out of his ass when I saw him at the meeting my pops had scheduled that week. Since everything with the drop had gone off without a hitch, we were on go mode for the next one. The guns we had were all military grade shit that we were planning to sell to the mafia and other drug organizations. I was going to make sure I set aside a couple for me too though, because I did it with every shipment, just in case shit got real for us. In the meantime, I ordered me some food and after changing my sheets, I got comfortable back in the bed.

SHAI A'SANTI

S hit was making perfect sense now all of a sudden. Zuri had played it cool at the doctor's office and hadn't given away that she knew me or that she was bothered by me being there with Kendra, but I saw that shit all in her eyes. I hadn't taken her for the type to keep a nigga's baby away, but I guess bitches surprised you every day. What she didn't know was that I wasn't just some regular ass nigga, so finding her wasn't going to be a problem. Scrolling through my phone, I sent a picture of her and her name to a hacker bitch I knew named Elle. She could find out anything for the right price and I was ready to pay whatever to find Zuri's sneaky ass. When I got the confirmation text back, I finished getting dressed and headed out to Suave, the restaurant that nobody knew I owned. I needed something to keep my mind occupied and off of all the bullshit that had been thrown at me in the last twenty-four hours.

"Hi, Mr. A'santi," the hostess greeted me as soon as I walked in. I dipped my head in a nod but kept walking, doing the same to the waitresses and waiters on the way to my office. My manager Carla was sitting behind the desk looking annoyed, but the second I walked in her face split into a smile.

"Shai, what you doin' in my neck of the woods?" She immediately got up and started cleaning up the papers she'd been looking over.

"Suave is *my* neck of the woods Carla, so I can come and go as I please." My stern tone had her eyeing me and she quickly picked up on my mood.

"I didn't mean—is everything okay?"

"It's fine, just take your things to *your* office so I can sit in mine, please." She looked like she was on the verge of tears as she rushed to grab the rest of her things and hurried out of the room. Feeling like an asshole, but not enough to apologize, I shut the door behind her and took a seat. Just like every other time I was there though, it wasn't long before someone was knocking on my door.

"Come in."

"Uhhhh, Mr. A'santi, there's a man here for you and he, uh, says he's your father," Carla's scary ass said in a hushed tone. How the nigga even knew where I was, was beyond me. I'd just told his ass the day before that I wasn't fucking with him, yet he'd found his way into my establishment to further harass me. Not wanting to cause a scene, I followed her out front to where my father was seated at a table alone while two men stood nearby, surprising me. Nodding for her to go, I took a seat and steepled my fingers together on the table. I couldn't deny that me and this nigga looked alike, aside from his greasy ass hair and green eyes. It was crazy that no one besides my family knew of our relation when I had his whole face, but I'd learned people were willfully ignorant and chose to believe what they wanted.

"What you want from me, man?" I elected not to even ask how he'd known I was there and just got straight to the point.

His eyes shifted and he let out a heavy sigh. "I want a relationship with you. My father Giorgiano is on his death bed and about to hand down everything to me. I can now make the rules and live how I want, and I would like to begin building our bond and repairing what I've broken." I tried not to, but laughter erupted from deep within my stomach, drawing stares from my staff and customers alike.

"That's the bullshit ass story you wanna run with? Okay, say I do believe that you wanna make things different. Ain't no way you can change a hundred-year-old rule just because you want to, and furthermore, what exactly do you think we gone do? Toss footballs around and shit? I'm a grown ass man, damn near about to have my own children! There ain't shit you can offer me that I want, not even your time, now if you'll excuse me, I have a business to run." I was already on my feet about to walk away from his ass, hopefully for good, but his next words stopped me in my tracks.

"I'm trying to offer you a seat at the table, son. Equal power, equal money, equal ties. I'm trying to offer you your birthright." Turning around, I studied him to see if he was serious and was surprised to see that he was being genuine. I took a few smooth steps back over to the table and saw him visibly relax.

"And *you*, a man who couldn't even tell his family that he had a black son, can promise me this?" I questioned lowly, and he raised his hands.

"I swear on my mother, the authority is now mine." I rolled the idea around in my head briefly about what a seat at the throne would mean for me and my family. Unlimited funds, unlimited protection, we would be kings. I immediately realized that this was the way he'd gotten back in good with Queen. All she'd ever wanted was for me to claim my spot in the De'Luca family, and now with Giorgiano dying it was within arm's reach. As tempting as the offer sounded, I needed to think it over more. I couldn't just get in bed with a nigga that was willing to abandon his own seed for decades. I needed to weigh the pros and cons.

"I'll consider it, but in the meantime, don't contact me," I warned before walking off.

&.

I spent the day crunching numbers and ordering things that the restaurant needed as I mulled over the idea of being a head in the De'Luca mafia. When Elle finally messaged me with the information on Zuri, I was already on my way out the door and smirked at her perfect timing. Her job was closed so it was safe to assume she was home, and that's exactly where I was headed. *Fuck if her nigga was there.*

I took a minute to go over her information and laughed seeing that she was already married when her ass was in Miami. *Sneaky ass!* The only thing saving her from my real wrath was the fact that there were two addresses listed for her, one being a home with both her and her husband's names on it and the other more recent one with just hers. Further inspection showed that she'd filed for divorce not too long after returning from her trip, and some of the irritation I was feeling went away. At least she'd made some attempt at moving away from that nigga, even though it still didn't explain why she was with him at the doctor's office booed up.

Tossing my phone aside, I made the half-hour drive to her condo and nodded in approval at how nice they were. Of course, if it was confirmed that she was my baby mama, she was moving expeditiously, but we still had a while to figure that out. Spotting the car out front that Elle had listed for her, I parked next to it and got out, straightening my suit. For some reason I wanted to make sure I was presentable, even though I wanted to wring her slender ass neck.

As I made it closer to the door, I could hear her talking loudly and it swung open before I could even knock. Her and the lady I assumed was her mama both stared at me with different expressions on their faces. Zuri looked completely stunned and her mama looked like she wanted to take me down.

"Shaaaaaiii," she dragged, forcing an uncomfortable smile. "What are you—how do you know where I live?" Her voice was high-pitched as her mama gave her the side-eye.

"I have my ways." Smirking, I looked her up and down trying

to see if anything was different about her, but all that had changed was her face looking just a little chubbier. She actually looked good enough to eat in the tight-fitting, maroon lounge set she wore.

"Well, don't be rude and leave your friend out there, Zuri." Her mama pushed her aside and waved me in, smiling hard. "I'm Zora, Zuri's mother," she gushed, introducing herself as she guided me further inside. It was obvious Zuri lived there alone judging from the light ass girly colors all over. Without being invited to, I took a seat while Zuri stood in the doorway with wide eyes.

Her mother rushed to the kitchen to bring me something to drink, leaving us alone and I wasted no time getting right to the point. "You pregnant?" Her body language told on her before she could try to lie as she instinctively wrapped her arms around her stomach. Seeing me follow the action she sighed deeply and leaned against the door frame.

"Yes."

"Is it mine?" Her pretty ass face balled up and her body tensed.

"No! I don't know!" she caught herself. "We were pretty careful in Miami but we had a couple of slip ups so I'm not sure." Shame had her eyes shifting to the corner of the room and I released a breath I didn't know I was holding.

"Look, I'm not here to judge you or no shit like that. I just don't want another nigga possibly raising my kid while I'm—"

"Out raising your other one?" she cut in, hinting at Kendra, and I chuckled bitterly. Since she hadn't given me any details about being a whole ass married woman, I wasn't going to tell her my business either. Besides, the only thing she needed to concern herself about was whether or not her baby was mine.

"My children will both be taken care of, that's the whole reason why I sought you out when I found out you might be expecting." She looked like she wanted to probe further, but her mama came back carrying a bottle of water for me and a glass of wine for herself.

"Here you go Shai, it's nice and cold too." She sat down on the couch next to me, waiting while I took a sip as if she'd spiked the shit.

"Dang Ma, what about me?" Zuri huffed, and Zora waved her off.

"You know where everything at," she said, not even looking her way. "Soooo, how do you know my baby girl, Shai?" Zuri was headed to the kitchen but the question had her pausing to wait on my response, and I smirked.

"Actually, I met her a few months ago in Miami," I hinted with a shrug.

"Zuri, you didn't tell me anything about meeting somebody —ohhhh, y'all two?" Finally catching on, Zora's eyes shifted between the two of us before her face grew tight. "Give me my damn water back, nigga! I oughta fuck you up! Is he the reason you was actin' like that in the doctor's office?"

Zuri nodded sheepishly and Zora groaned. "Lord, my baby a thot! Girl, how you come home with two baby daddies? I'm bouta go 'cause this is too much!" she huffed, setting down our drinks and storming to the door before whipping around. "And don't even think about trying none of that fatal attraction shit or I'ma come find yo' ass myself!"

I threw my hands up in surrender, trying hard to keep a straight face as she left. "Now why would you do that? I didn't want my mama to know—"

"That you was out in Miami poppin' that pussy for a real nigga?" I cracked, and she sucked her teeth irritably. "She was going to find out anyway if the baby came out light bright, don't you think?"

"You got jokes, but this is serious!"

"Oh, I know, and believe me when I say *I'm* serious about being involved until we know that that's your husband's baby and not mine." Just like with Kendra, I was giving her the chance to be up front with me. Whether or not she wanted to take it was completely up to her, but I figured she didn't want me to tell that nigga I might be the daddy.

"Okay."

"Okay?" I couldn't deny my surprise at how easy it had been to pin her ass down. Kendra barely wanted me to come to her appointments at first, I had to bully my way in them. Just like before though, Zuri was one upping her ass without even trying.

"*Yes, okay.* Right now they have me going to the doctor every week since I've had complications in the past, so honestly you may not even have to worry about any of this." The sadness in her voice had me crossing the room swiftly. Despite how upset I was with her for being secretive, I didn't like her speaking that shit into existence.

"Hey, don't say no shit like that, ayite?" I lifted her chin, looking deeply into her eyes. "This baby gone be perfect, full term, and probably gone weigh like ten pounds."

We both chuckled as I thumbed away the lone tear on her cheek. "That's not funny! Don't you wish that evil on me!" Sniffling, she gave me a weak shove that didn't move me an inch.

"I'm just saying, whether this my baby or not, I want you to have a happy, healthy pregnancy, so whatever you need me to do, I will," I vowed, meaning every word. Even if we found out it wasn't my baby, I was going to look out since it was clear her bitch ass husband wasn't. There was no reason why she should've been nervous about her pregnancy because he should've been there reassuring her. It was cool though, because I was stepping in.

ZURI MILLER

The pressure of telling Shai had been lifted off my shoulders and I was honestly surprised by how easily he had accepted the news. I was sure that Deshawn wasn't going to be anywhere near as understanding when I told him, even though his ass had a whole live-in girlfriend. I figured it'd be best to tell him before my next appointment though, so he wouldn't cause a scene and stress me out. Then again, for him to have been so excited at the appointment, I hadn't heard a peep out of his ass since then. I wasn't going to press him to be a part of my baby's life though, Shai either. I was quickly learning that niggas talked a good game but they oftentimes disappointed you. So now I was taking everything with a grain of salt to keep my stress down.

I was on my way to meet Sevyn at Let's Eat To Live restaurant for some good food and to catch her up on Shai popping up on me. Since there wasn't much I could do now, we'd decided to start meeting for lunch or dinner every week for the rest of my pregnancy. I'd seen this place on TikTok and had been dying to go ever since. It was easy to talk Sevyn's greedy ass into going and once she saw the video, she was thirsty to go too.

I found a decent parking spot and waited for her to call and let me know she'd made it, when a text came through from Shai asking if I'd eaten yet. The night he came over we exchanged information and he'd been texting or calling me every day since. Unable to stop the smile that crossed my face, I hurried to let his nosy ass know I was meeting Sevyn right then. A second later, a notification popped up that he'd sent me a thousand dollars for food, and I immediately called him.

"Sir, it's not one place me and Sevyn can go to spend all this," I said as soon as he answered.

"Good, you can spend whatever's left on something nice for yourself or the baby." I could hear that he was smiling as well and my heart fluttered. I needed to chill, we'd only just had a conversation the other day and I was already completely smitten with him again. He'd explained that the woman I saw him with was an ex that he'd broken up with *before* Miami because she was cheating on him, and when she found out she was pregnant he stepped up as a man to be there for her since she refused to give him a DNA test. That made my heart melt even more and I was like putty, but I was keeping it as cool as possible so I wouldn't hurt my own feelings with my expectations.

"Awww, thank you," I gushed, already making a mental note to start up a bank account for the baby. Deshawn had known for a week and hadn't given me anything or mentioned the future. I understood he was probably just being cautious after the last time, but it still hurt to know he was waiting for something to happen or not happen.

"Don't worry about it, just enjoy yourself," he said nonchalantly before we said our goodbyes. I was still cheesing when I got off the phone and saw Sevyn walking toward my car.

"Only crazy people sit alone in their cars smiling, Zee," she teased as I climbed out.

"I was on the phone, hoe." I rolled my eyes playfully as we headed toward the entrance.

"Oh, I'ma need this tea for real now 'cause I know weak ass Deshawn ain't got you chinnin' and grinnin' like that."

"Okay, I won't lie, I was talkin' to Shai and when I told him I was out eating with you that nigga sent me a stack." I was still in disbelief that he'd done it and Sevyn's face said she was too.

"Okaaaay! Friend better come through with that BDE! He need to give some to his crazy ass cousin 'cause all that nigga do is bring me food. I'm convinced his ass tryna make me fat." Her nose wrinkled as she spoke, and I nodded knowingly.

"Mmmhmm, so you gone finally admit y'all still been messing around?" She froze up before looking away with a smile.

"You got me." She nudged me with her shoulder as we made it to the door and waited to be seated. "That nigga just sooo *nasty*." She shuddered and I could've sworn she moaned, making me give her ass the side eye.

"Uhhh, don't be making them nasty noises in these people's restaurant." I laughed but I was low key jealous for real. The last sex I'd had was with Shai months ago and although it was spine-tingling good, I was all the way backed up three months later, so I couldn't even relate.

"I'm just saying." Shrugging, she checked her phone before meeting my eyes. "The sex is great and he's sweet when he wants to be, but I can already tell it's going to be an issue with him keeping things quiet, if you know what I mean."

I knew exactly what she meant, but my brows dipped anyway as I tried to figure out why that would be a problem. In my opinion, Tramel was being selfish if he was requiring her to remain loyal for fifteen more years. I'd told her that ,but Sevyn was way too loyal. She felt like him risking his freedom to buy her shop was enough of a reason to remain tied to him, but I'd only just gotten out of a tumultuous marriage, so what did I know.

"I mean, do you even still love and plan to be with Tramel or is this all about loyalty for you? 'Cause you might be blocking your blessings." She got quiet, seemingly considering my question. I knew it wasn't something she could just decide right that second, but I hoped she give it some thought before she lost her youth waiting on that nigga.

"Girl, when you get so smart?" she joked. "Let me find out all I need to figure out the mysteries of the world is to get knocked up."

"Naw, I wouldn't suggest that boo. I'm just now starting to feel better since they gave me that medicine to help with nausea."

"Oh, well naw, 'cause I love food way too much for that." We shared a laugh as someone came over and led us to a table. There were so many things on the menu that I wanted to try, I knew I'd be back just so I could sample it all. Like I'd told Sevyn, I'd only just been able to eat normally so I wasn't trying to tempt fate.

I ended up ordering the lamb with greens and baked macaroni while Sevyn got the red snapper and coconut sweet rice. While we waited for the food, I filled her in on how my divorce proceedings were going, which was nowhere fast. The baby had only given Deshawn even more of a reason to fight things and I was truly fed up with him.

"He's so annoying. How he got a whole woman living in y'all house and won't give you a divorce?"

"Tell me about it," I grumbled, taking a sip of my water.

"You should tell Shai, I bet he'd make his ass sign them papers," her crazy ass said. I'd only just started talking to Shai again and had already roped him into my shit enough, so telling him about my issues with my estranged husband would be doing too much. I immediately shook my head.

"Hell no, for one ,Shai would eat Deshawn's little ass for breakfast, and for two, I don't need to involve him in no more of my drama. I already just told the man I don't know if he's my baby daddy from our little tryst. The last thing I want to do is add a crazy ass husband and his mistress in this shit."

"Well hell, those are the exact reasons why you should tell him!" she cackled. "I'd pay good money to see that fight." I couldn't help but laugh with her as I imagined the way Shai would beat Deshawn's ass.

"You're mean as hell."

"Shit, you're mean too 'cause you think it's funny." She

humped her shoulder as our food was brought to the table, and everything smelled so amazing our conversation instantly ceased.

We wasted no time digging in and the food was definitely as good as TikTok said it was. By the time we left I was good and stuffed, carrying a to-go tray just like Sevyn. I planned to go home and take a nap then wake up and eat again on some truly greedy shit.

"Okay, let me get this food back to Tyrese's whiny ass," Sevyn said, giving me a side hug and air kisses. "I'm gone call you later."

"Okay, bye boo."

I waited until she was safely in her car before pulling off and heading back to my house. I only had one more day off and I intended to get as much rest as I could, but the second I pulled up, I rolled my eyes seeing a call from my dad. My first mind told me to ignore that shit and finish enjoying my day, but I firmly believed in cherishing my parents while they were alive, no matter how irritating they were.

"Hey Dad," I greeted as I climbed out of my car with my tray in hand.

"Hey baby, how you doin'?"

"I'm good, just got back from a late lunch with Sevyn. How are you?" I balanced everything I was carrying as I made my way up to my door and let myself in.

"Ohhh, that's good. I'm doin' okay though, just was calling to check on you." I immediately knew his ass was lying, but I didn't call him out. "I actually just got some exciting news I wanna share with you." *Here he goes*, I thought, hoping that his news didn't have shit to do with Deshawn.

"Oh okay, well I'm all ears." Walking further inside, I set my things down and took a seat on the couch to await his news. He paused, sighing for a moment, and I got slightly worried, immediately thinking the worst.

"Uhh, listen, I just found out you might have a sister." Stunned, I plopped down on the couch trying to process what he'd said. "This would've been before me and your mama got together, so don't think I was cheating on her." He hurried to try and explain before I could speak.

"So, when exactly was this? Who is this woman and how did she all of a sudden find you after all these years?" I found myself asking defensively. I needed to know specifics because he couldn't have thought he'd just drop this shit in my lap and not further explain.

"This was in high school back in California, before I moved here, Zuri. I guess she decided to look me up on Facebook. Isn't that how everybody finds people nowadays?"

"Wow," was the only thing that I could think to say. I was so dumbfounded.

"I'm going to meet her tomorrow, but I won't know for sure until we take the DNA test and if it's confirmed, then I'd like you two to meet," my dad told me like it was the most normal thing in the world for his old ass to still be taking paternity tests. Just to get him off the phone, I agreed and hung up, wishing I could have some wine after that mess. At my age I didn't know how me and some new sister would even get along. Hell, what if her and her mama were scammers? It was way too much to consider and I wasn't going to let it stress me out, but I was going to talk to my mama about it ASAP.

SHAI A'SANTI

Zuri had finally decided to tell her bitch ass husband about the baby possibly not being his. She also thought it would be best if I was there so when her next appointment rolled around he wouldn't be blindsided and cause a scene at the doctor's office. I agreed mostly because I wanted to see the look on his face when he realized I'd slid up in his wife *raw*, but also because I didn't want him to do shit to her if she was alone with him. Some men's egos were fragile as fuck and finding out that a baby he thought they made might be someone else's was sure to make his ass act a fool. I wanted to be there to beat his ass if necessary since I was sure she didn't want me to have to kill him.

Pulling up to Zuri's, I made sure my safety was off my gun before getting out and making my way up to her door. Seconds after knocking she was pulling the door open with her nerves showing on her face. She breathed a visible sigh of relief when she saw it was me though. It felt good knowing she was so comfortable with me, but it also meant she was way too worried about that nigga.

"Hey, I thought Deshawn came early since I didn't see your car." She gave me a brief hug, trying to discreetly peek around me before stepping back to let me in.

"Yeah, I have a few different cars, but you'll know them all soon," I let her know with confidence. Unable to stop myself, I eyed her thick frame, noting how effortlessly beautiful she was. Most women would've been completely done up knowing that two men they'd had sex with we're going to be in the same room, but not Zuri. She'd opted to comfortable in baggy maroon sweatpants and a graphic tee. Her hair was up in a huge puff ball with curly tendrils framing her face and neck and she was completely barefaced. I didn't know which way I liked to see her most at this point, because I'd been around her in full glam mode and dressed down and she killed both looks with ease.

"Oh, okay, well I'm glad you're here first because I'd like to talk to you about something." Her response to me mentioning my array of cars wasn't something I was used to. Any other woman I'd dealt with, including Kendra, had noted each time I showed up in something different. That shit held no weight with Zuri and it only drew me to her even more.

She led me to the living room, turning to face me once we finally made it. Seeing how nervous she was had me stepping in her space and lifting her chin, unable to stop myself from touching her. "Hey, what's wrong?" I was fully prepared to handle whatever was bothering her, especially when I saw her eyes glistening.

"I uh... I just want you know how much I appreciate the way you've stepped up for me with no questions asked. This whole situation is pretty crazy and you could've just said fuck me until this baby gets here, but you didn't and that means a lot to me."

"You don't gotta thank me for doing what I'm supposed to. We both knew the risks in Miami, so being here is a given and whatever you need, it's yours. I already told you that and I mean it, no matter what the outcome is." I stroked her cheek tenderly, and before I could fight it I lowered my head, capturing her lips in a soft kiss.

I already knew I was fucking up because I wasn't supposed to be going there with Zuri, especially when we both had so much baggage, but she made it hard to deny her. It had been some months since I'd been inside of her and my dick remembered everything about how tight and wet her pussy was. With one arm around her waist, I toyed with the band of her sweats, easily reaching inside and cupping her pussy through the fabric of her panties. She was already soaking through the material and I slipped my fingers past them, instantly coming in contact with her protruding clit.

Sucking in a breath, Zuri spread her thighs, allowing me even more access to her slippery center. "Shai, we caaaaaan't," she whined even as she moved her hips, riding my fingers.

"Why not?" I was ready to take her right there in her living room my dick was so hard, but as if on cue, there was a knock at the door. Zuri instantly tried to pull away, but I held her firmly in place, making her eyes buck as I continued playing in her wetness.

"Shai—" she tried weakly, but I only sped up, adding more friction to my movements.

"What, you deserve this nut and you gone get it. Fuck that nigga, he can wait," I growled against her lips, feeling her body beginning to convulse as she fell against me, unable to stop the orgasm coming on.

"Ohhh shiiiit!"

"Let that shit go," I ordered, pleased when her pussy began pulsating in my hand as she filled it with her sweet juices. I held her up, allowing her to ride the wave of her orgasm until she finally stopped jerking. Removing my fingers, I stuck them right in my mouth, licking them clean, and smirked. "Good girl."

It took another few seconds for her to gather herself enough to go and clean herself up. I went to the kitchen to wash my hands while she headed to her room to change and the whole time, this nigga was still outside knocking. She came back quick as hell, this time wearing a pair of navy-blue sweats and despite her haste, I could see that she was much more relaxed. I sat down on the couch while she let that nigga in, and I could already hear his bitch ass complaining about having to wait, but he shut up instantly when he saw me. He looked between the two of us angrily as his mind began to wander, and I smirked, only confirming whatever it was he was thinking.

"Who the fuck is this, Zuri! I know damn well you ain't call me over here while you fuckin' a whole nigga in this bitch!" He turned his rage to her, not wanting any parts of my two-hundred-thirty-pound frame, but if he thought he was about to talk to her crazy then he was even more of a fool than I thought.

"Aye, use lowercase letters talking to her!" I hissed, standing up. He snapped his head in my direction and the tight expression he wore softened some.

He addressed Zuri with his eyes still on me. "Is this nigga yo' real baby daddy?"

"Deshawn—"

"Shit, I might be." I smirked sinisterly at the way his face dropped. As scared as he was to turn his back on me, he looked back at Zuri with an angry snort.

"You *been* fuckin' him?" He sounded hurt, and I wanted to laugh at his bitch ass.

"No, I met Shai back in Miami and—"

"So, you was out there with a nigga?" Chuckling bitterly, he shook his head. "You out here being a hoe with a nigga that already got somebody pregnant, but you're trying to divorce me? Bitch!" He lunged at her and I quickly yanked his little ass back by his shirt, making him fall to the floor as I took a stance in front of Zuri.

Growling, he shot back toward us and I didn't hesitate to hit his bitch ass with a swift right that had him stumbling. Before he could regain his composure, I had my nine in his face and he froze, looking between the two of us in disgust as blood dripped from his nose, and Zuri screamed.

"Shai!"

"You know what, fuck you! You can have this bitch!" he spat, swiping his hand across his face and storming out after giving us one last death stare.

"Oh my god," Zuri gasped from behind me in disbelief. "What the fuck just happened?" She seemed surprised even though we both knew his ass wasn't going to take the news well. Tucking my gun away, I turned to see her face buried in her hands as she cried, and I couldn't help feeling bad. Despite the circumstances, Zuri had been trying to do the right thing and that nigga had completely showed his ass.

"Stop crying before you stress the baby out," I told her, wrapping my arms around her shuddering body. "If that nigga tryna miss out on this baby because of this shit, then fuck him. I already told you I got you, and I meant that," I vowed, holding her until she eventually calmed down. Just to make sure she was good, I stuck around for a while. We ordered some food and chilled until she fell into a food coma, then I took the opportunity to leave. I had a few moves to make but I planned to return just to check on her again. Having ran off the other potential father, I really had to make sure Zuri and the baby were taken care of and I intended to do just that.

The day of Zuri's next appointment arrived fast and her bitch ass husband wasn't anywhere in sight. I'd been expecting for him to do some shit like that, but Zuri seemed surprised and hurt that he'd turn his back on her. She hid it well during her appointment, even when the doctor gave us curious stares because she knew Zuri's ass was married to another nigga but asking for a test from me. I dared her unprofessional ass to say something that would make Zuri feel any type of way, but she smartly kept her opinion to herself.

Since all it took for us to test the baby was a blood draw from Zuri and a mouth swab from me, we went ahead and got it done. They said it would only take a week for the results so by the time her next appointment rolled around, we'd know for sure. So far, everything seemed to be going fine with the baby though, and after telling her to continue taking her vitamins we were free to go.

"You wanna eat?" I found myself asking as we walked from the building together.

"Sure." She smiled, still heading to her car, but I quickly guided her toward mine. There was no need in driving separate and I didn't want to leave her presence anyway. She requested Texas Roadhouse which was right down the street basically and I quickly agreed ready to feed her ass whatever she wanted for some of her time.

I made the short drive to the restaurant and helped her out of the car, keeping her hand locked in mine as we walked to the door. It was mid-day so the place was packed but we were still able to find a table. We were browsing the menus even though I already knew what I wanted when I felt a presence over my shoulder and looked up to see Kendra. Her eyes were locked on Zuri who still hadn't noticed her as she damn near shook with anger.

"Who the fuck is this Shai?" she asked in a high-pitched voice that had Zuri looking up from her menu. Steepling my fingers together on top of the table I stared at her, silently trying to warn her to behave before introducing the two.

"Kendra this is Zuri, Zuri this is Kendra."

"Do you know that I'm pregnant?" Kendra wasted no time asking with her nose turned up. "Aren't you the lady from the doctor's office? So, you knew he was with me and still decided to see him?" she quizzed placing her hand on her hip to make her belly even more prominent in the coat she wore as if that would make a difference. I was sure she expected Zuri to back down, but instead she smirked.

"Congratulations, our baby's will be siblings so we should probably get to know each other. Wanna join us?"

"What!" Kendra shrieked turning her angry glare my way. I still had yet to tell her about Zuri's pregnancy, so she was blind-sided by the news and obviously pissed. "you got this bitch pregnant!" she was already drawing the attention of a few of the other customers near us and I narrowed my eyes trying hard to keep my cool.

"Watch yo' fuckin' mouth Ken." I warned making her shrink a bit. "you're not even sure that baby is mine and won't take a test so you don't have no room to question me. Take yo' ass back to wherever the fuck you just came from before I embarrass you." She stood mugging us both before storming out of the restaurant and I went right back to my menu avoiding Zuri's questioning stare.

Kendra could play crazy all she wanted but she was the one who'd made things the way they were and she was only making it worse by denying me a DNA. She wanted to throw her weight around and try to intimidate Zuri but she'd fumbled me on her own and whether the baby was mine or not I wasn't fucking with her. I was glad that even though she wanted to Zuri didn't further ruin our meal by probing me about that bitch. Honestly, Kendra was in the back of my mind before she'd even left and I wanted to keep it that way.

SEVYN ELLIS

I t was finally the day of my visit with Tramel and I had been on pins and needles since the night before. Zuri had really put some shit on my mind asking me about whether I wanted to be with him or not and after a long evaluation I realized that I didn't. I'd only been holding on to what I was used to because of a sense of guilt and loyalty that was all manipulation on Tramel's part. My love for him had long since dwindled and the only thing keeping us bonded was my shop and the looming sense that I owed him. I planned to tell him that I was done, and had gone over what I'd say a million times but I knew nothing I said was going to be taken well by him. No matter what Tramel was going to feel like I was betraying him and I couldn't help fearing what his response would be. He was a street nigga through and through and lived by the code that if you weren't with me then you were against me so he'd immediately consider me an enemy and that wasn't something I wanted to be. I wanted him to love me enough to *want* me to be happy and if my freedom was happiness then he'd willingly oblige, but I was starting to see that his ass didn't love me at all. He owned me.

I fidgeted as I sat at the table waiting for him and the other inmates to enter and when the doors opened, and they began

filing inside my heart slammed against my chest. Standing, I tried
to force a smile but I was sure it looked more like a grimace as I
spotted him in the back of the line. He on the other hand looked
pleased, taking in the skintight jeans and hoodie I had on with a
sexy smirk.

It was crazy that I used to be so smitten by his brown skinned
ass. I thought I was the luckiest girl ever to be his main, but now I
was seeing it was a prison that I wished I'd allowed another bitch
to be locked up in.

"Damn baby, you look good as fuck." His complimented
huskily, pulling me into a tight hug and squeezing my ass. He
went to press a kiss against my lips and I turned my head giving
him my cheek. The action had him looking at me hard as he
released me, since we only ever had a few seconds to make physical
contact in the beginning of a visit before the guards would put a
stop to it. I dropped onto the hard seat and he took his time doing
the same as he glared at me across the table, clearly feeling the
disconnect. "what the fuck wrong with you?" he asked folding his
hands and I chose to focus my gaze on them since he was looking
at me like he was going to kill my ass.

"Nothin' I uhh wanted to talk to you though."

"About what? Something happen at the shop?" that was all he
was worried about. His precious business and money. I resisted
the urge to scoff and finally met his deep brown eyes forcing
myself to get out the words that had been swimming in my mind
for weeks.

"No, I want a divorce."

Once I said it, I felt much better even as a silence settled over
us that should have been a warning to me. It was like he hadn't
even heard what I said because his expression never changed and
then he suddenly busted out laughing instantly taking me aback.

"A divorce? Ain't no divorcing Sevyn, you know that." his
laughter stopped short and he mugged me evilly. "You're *mine*
and the only way out this shit is death. You ready to die tryna be
with that lil' nigga?" the question had my heart leaping into my

throat. "Yeaaaah, I know everything, and I see everything, even behind these walls baby. I wasn't gone trip about you getting yo' little rocks off, but now you're letting that nigga cloud yo' judgement."

With a swiftness I wasn't expecting, he gripped my hands in his and squeezed them so tight tears sprang to my eyes. "Quit fuckin' playin' with me before I kill yo' stupid ass Sev. Ain't no divorcin'. Now smile and act like you happy to see a nigga, it's been a minute since you came through."

Forcing my lips to spread into a smile, I tried to blink back my tears as he sat back releasing my hands with a smile of his own. Inside I was burning up but I put on the biggest front as he changed the subject to business completely unfazed by the shit he'd just done and said. I spent the next two hours pretending that I wanted to be there and when it was finally time to go, he didn't allow me to move away before shoving his tongue down my throat. Evilly, I wished I'd sucked Zaakir's dick before coming since his ass insisted on kissing me.

"Remember what the fuck I said. Don't be out there tryna commit suicide Sevyn." Were his last words to me, before grinning sinisterly and getting in line. Glad the visit was finally over, I wasted no time getting the fuck out of there, only feeling like I could breathe again once I was behind the wheel of my car. It took all of ten minutes for me to get my heart rate back under control and when I did I reached for my constantly buzzing phone. I had multiple texts from Tyrese, a few calls from Zuri and one from Zaakir. Only Tyrese knew about what I was going to do that day and I didn't want to tell him how things had gone, I also didn't want to have Zuri questioning me about what was wrong when she heard it in my voice. Despite Tramel's warning, I opted to call Zaakir back.

"Damn, where you been girl? I normally would've heard from yo' thirsty ass at least twice already." Unable to stop myself I chuckled noting how he was trying to play off his concern.

"Awww you sound like you missed me?" I teased, finally starting my car and pulling out of the lot.

"Maybe a lil' bit but I'm tryna feed and fuck you so where you at?" I really should've been being cautious considering the threat that Tramel had just made, but I wasted no time telling him to meet me at his house. I was in need of a release and some good food and I knew Zaakir was going to deliver both. *Fuck Tramel!*

§.

It had been a week since my visit with Tramel and I'd still been hanging heavy with Zaakir as if the man hadn't threatened my life. Somehow being with Zaakir made me feel like no one else existed not even my husband and that was mostly because his ass didn't. Tyrese thought I should've been being more careful after I told him what all was said during our visit but I wasn't trying to hear that shit. Tramel could talk all he wanted but the truth was, his ass was behind bars and doing anything to me wasn't good for him because his money flowed through me.

Locking up my shop, I pulled out my phone to let Zaakir know I was on my way. I'd had a last-minute walk in that had taken much longer than I expected so everybody had already cleared out. I wasn't tripping because the three hundred dollars was worth the extra hour and a half of work. Zaakir texted right back, telling me to hurry up and I sucked my teeth as I involuntarily picked up speed.

"Hey Sevyn!" I turned around at the sound of my name and came face to face with a gun. Instantly my hands flew up and I prepared to offer the man every dime I had. "Tramel said til death do y'all part!"

Pow! Pow!

Zuri Ross

I hadn't heard from Deshawn since he'd stormed out of my house and I couldn't say that it wasn't a relief. I'd been stress free in his absence and my baby was thriving which made me even more happy about the distance. Shai had been picking up his slack anyway, so it was like he didn't even exist. The only problem was that I didn't know if I could fully trust him. He'd said that he would be there no matter what, but I couldn't help worrying a little at the possibility that he'd switch up if the test said he wasn't the father. Seeing the way he'd done his other baby mama let me know exactly what it was like to be on his bad side and I wasn't trying to put myself in that situation. Thankfully, the guessing game would be over soon because it was the day we were supposed to be getting our results back.

"Sit down before you burn a hole in yo' carpet." Shai cracked from his seat on my couch. He'd come over so we could read the results together and was surprisingly chill while I was about to have a panic attack.

"Shut up." I giggled but stopped the steady trek I'd been making across the floor. Reaching out for me, Shai pulled me onto the couch next to him and sighed.

"You stressin' for nothin'. I keep tellin' you, I'ma be here regardless so relax." he shrugged and I couldn't help marveling at how fine he was. Noticing how hard I was staring he licked his lips sexily. "You want me to put my face in yo' pussy? Will that make you feel better?"

As nervous as I was, my thighs instantly clenched together. Since the day that he'd brought me to climax in my living room, we hadn't come close to fucking again despite me being horny as hell. It was like the baby had my sex drive on one thousand and I wanted it all the time, but I couldn't bring myself to ask him again. Liquid courage had been the main reason I'd been able to do so in the beginning but since I couldn't drink that wasn't an option.

Before I could tell him that I'd very much like that, my phone chimed and then his did a second later. My eyes widened and my heart pounded seeing an email from my doctor's office and Shai lifted his phone so I could see that he got the same thing.

"You open it."

"Gone head and open it."

We spoke at the same time and a nervous chuckle escaped me. I was glad when he sighed, and opened his silently reading over whatever it said while I looked on tensely. "What, what does it say!" I asked frantically when he mumbled a low damn under his breath. Turning the screen so I could see it, I read the multiple row of nines and threw my arms around him.

"Looks like you're stuck with me for at least eighteen years," he said giving me a little squeeze.

I hadn't even realized how badly I wanted Shai to be the father until that moment and I couldn't have been happier that he was. Before I knew it, my lips captured his first giving light pecks and then our tongues were entwined. He pulled me into his lap, cupping my ass in both hands as our kiss deepened. I could already feel my wetness soaking the seat of my panties and I moaned lowly in anticipation as Shai grew hard beneath me.

He wasted no time standing up with me still in his arms and my scary ass tightened my hold on him afraid that he'd drop me but he headed toward my bedroom with ease. Setting me on my feet he continued kissing me even as he removed each article of clothing I had on until I was standing before him completely naked. Just like in Miami the lust in his eyes had my clit throbbing. "get on the bed." He ordered huskily. His quiet demanding tone and the look on his face had me jumping to do so. On my hands and knees, I climbed on the edge of the bed and sucked in a sharp breath when I felt his tongue slither its way between my folds. Frozen, I tooted my ass up giving him more access and he hungrily sucked my clit in his mouth.

"Shaaaaaiii," I moaned, throwing my head back as he devoured me. He gripped my ass cheeks pulling them apart and I grinded against his tongue. In no time I felt an orgasm rushing through my body and I gripped the sheets tightly. "Ohhhh fuck, I'm cuuuuuummmminnng!"

Grunting, he thumbed my asshole sending me over the edge and a gush of fluids came spilling out as my body convulsed. I fell forward still reeling, but he pulled me back onto my knees.

"I been waiting to get back in this pussy for months baby, don't tap out on me yet." With one hand holding me up, I could hear him unbuckling his belt and kicking off his jeans. In seconds he was stretching my walls with his big dick and I bit my lip at how good he felt. "God damn why yo' pussy so wet?" he groaned easing into me slowly. He bent down so that he could plant kisses on my neck and shoulder going deeper and deeper until I was sure he was tapping my uterus.

"Mmmfuck, baby!" my words came out jumbled as he reached around and teased my clit.

"I missed this Zee, I missed feeling you choking my dick to death with this lethal ass pussy! This my pussy now understand?"

Unable to form a word let alone a sentence, I could only nod as my eyes rolled into the back of my head. Between him talking and the rhythmic sound he was making as he slid through my walls, I was on the edge of erupting and I bit back another moan.

"You're mine right?" he demanded, pushing into me so deep I squealed.

"Yeeees! Yes I'm all yours!" my mouth hung open panting as I stretched to reach the orgasm that was fast approaching. "Baaaaby, fuck me!"

"I'm bouta nut Zee, shiiit. Can I nut in my pussy?" he wanted to know even though I could already feel him pulsing ready to release his seed in me.

"Yessss, nut all in me!" I sniveled as I reached my peak, once again squirting and soaking us both and my sheets. I heard him curse under his breath and his movements slowed down becoming more stiff and jerky as he filled me up, falling on top of me with a moan.

"Damn Zuri, I swear yo' pussy got crack in it, fuck." He rolled off of me breathing heavily as he fell onto his back.

"Well you got heroin in yo' dick so we're perfect," I said making him laugh. We laid there for a few minutes before my stomach growled.

"Let's get cleaned up and go grab some food." He was already up and helping me to stand even though my legs felt like jelly. Our shower ended up taking longer than expected because he just had to fuck me there too, and by the time we got out I almost didn't want to leave but our hungry baby wasn't trying to hear that. Shai threw back on his clothes while I slipped on some leggings and a long-sleeved crop top with a hoodie.

I couldn't lie, the sex had me feeling good and refreshed as we walked hand in hand into Suave. Shai had insisted I try it, promising that the Alfredo chicken I was craving was the best there. I hadn't even ever heard of the upscale restaurant, but I was willing to try anything once even though we were completely underdressed for the atmosphere. The hostess greeted us with a wide smile, and quickly grabbed two menus.

"Good evening Mr. A'santi, would you like your regular booth?" I giggled at the fact that he came there so often they knew him by name and had a regular booth for him and he smirked cockily.

"Yes that's fine thank you." Still smiling she led us through the dining area while Shai locked his hand in mine. Almost toward the back a familiar face had trying hard to hide but he recognized me immediately as we passed.

"Zuri?"

Pausing, I turned around and forced a smile on my face. "hey dad, what are you doing here?" he was so focused on Shai and our interlocked fingers that he could barely answer and I prayed he didn't say anything crazy.

"I'm having dinner, what are you doing here?" he eyed Shai with his face twisted and I rushed to introduce them.

"I'm here to eat too. This is my child's father, Shai, Shai this is my dad Kadeem." Neither man seemed interested in the other and instantly felt the tension between them, but I wasn't about to let their rudeness ruin my good sex mood or my dinner. "Wellll, we should get going—"

"Hold on, since you're here, you might as well meet your sister." He cheesed, looking just past us, and although I didn't like how he was putting me on the spot, I still put on a friendly smile. Instantly, that smile fell from my face as I locked eyes with Shai's ex. "Zuri, meet your big sister...Kendra."

To be continued...

ALSO BY J. DOMINIQUE

The Coldest Savage Stole My Heart 2

Made in United States
North Haven, CT
29 April 2024

51927641R00086